DANIEL
OF BABYLON

A Novel by Bob Jones

BOB JONES UNIVERSITY PRESS ● Greenville, SC 29614

Daniel of Babylon
by Bob Jones
© 1984 by Bob Jones University Press
Greenville, SC 29614
ISBN: 0-89084-270-1
All rights reserved

Printed in the United States of America

Dedicated to the History and Bible Departments of Bob Jones University with the hope that neither department will find in this book any cause for embarrassment.

The author is greatly obligated to Eva Carrier for her efficient research and wishes to express his sincere appreciation and gratitude to her.

Thanks are also due to Susan Bishop for her patience in copying and recopying the manuscript and preparing it for publication.

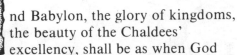 nd Babylon, the glory of kingdoms, the beauty of the Chaldees' excellency, shall be as when God overthrew Sodom and Gomorrah. It shall never be inhabited, neither shall it be dwelt in from generation to generation . . . . But wild beasts of the desert shall lie there; and their houses shall be full of doleful creatures; and owls shall dwell there, and satyrs shall dance there. And the wild beasts of the islands shall cry in their desolate houses, and dragons in their pleasant palaces.

Isaiah

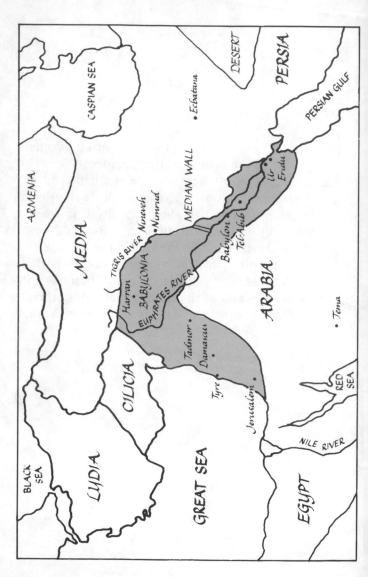

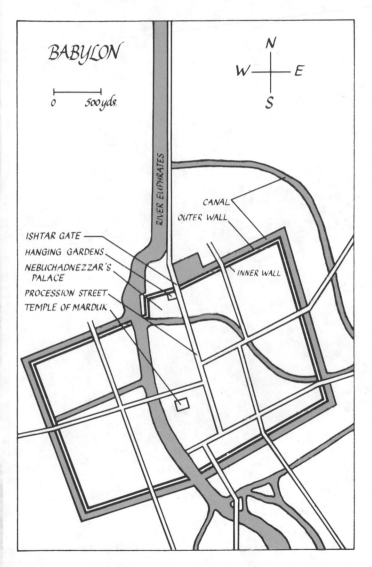

As I was led into the pavilion, I became aware of Nebuchadnezzar. It was impossible to avoid noticing him, dressed as he was in full regalia with his officers behind and on either side of his chair and the scribes and the notaries seated cross-legged on the carpets before him. This awareness was far more than merely noting the person of this great crown prince; it was a consciousness of strength, of power that emanated from him like a strong wind. It was tangible, this awareness.

I had watched this royal warrior from the walls as he, always in the forefront of the operation, supervised the siege of the city. To me then he had seemed like a general going about his business with thoroughness and determination but somehow like a man to whom war was a mere necessity— not an excitement of the senses and a career to be followed with enthusiasm. Though I had experienced similar feelings of entering, as it were, into men's souls, I can never remember one so distinct and strong as that which I now felt. I said to myself, "Perhaps you sense the king's power so

1

strongly because you have today come to manhood," for this was my sixteenth birthday; but I recognized that this impression was more than that. It was a sort of spiritual understanding, the exercise of a gift from God.

I was no stranger to the presence of kings. My uncle Jehoiakim had taken me three years before to live in his house upon the death of my mother, his sister. My father, too, had been of royal blood, though I could not remember him, as he had fallen in battle while I was still a young child. I knew the ways of a royal court, provincial though Judah may have been. Because of my youth and the pride of my heritage, I am sure I felt the humiliation of this occasion as keenly as any of the Jews standing there before our conqueror. Having spent two years training to become an officer in Jehoiakim's mounted guard, my dreams were of great battles, victories, and the expanding power of Judah. There was no preparation of my spirit for defeat.

The siege of Jerusalem had been brief. Unprepared as we were for the sudden arrival of the Babylonian army, short on stores and supplies, Jehoiakim was brought to a swift surrender. The statesmen of the city and the king himself had met for three days with the representatives of Nebuchadnezzar to work out the details of the surrender and the plans for the future of the city.

I wondered why Nebuchadnezzar had ordered Hananiah, Mishael, Azariah, and me to be present—three young men and Azariah, a boy of fourteen. The brothers, Hananiah and Mishael, like me, were wards of the king, distant cousins of King Jehoiakim. Azariah had been adopted as a mere baby by one of the royal princesses; and, of course, there were those who said he was her natural son.

Looking back over the full years that lie between that day and this, I suppose it is not surprising that I have such a vague memory of the details of that occasion. Yet I can still see clearly the purple tent curtains, stirred by the faint breeze, move in and out as if they were breathing entities. I still see, too, the worn spot in the carpet under Nebuchadnezzar's crimson boots—something I was not aware I noticed at all that day. I remember sharply, however, the surprise I felt when in the terms of the surrender it was stated that Hananiah, Mishael, Azariah, and I would be taken back with the conqueror to Babylon.

All of the preparations for departure, all of the excitement at the thought of what might lie ahead in great Babylon, could not remove the grief I felt at leaving my home. I loved everything about Jerusalem—the narrow streets, the busy marketplace, the armory and barracks, the palace, and the small home where I was born and passed my earliest years. Especially I loved the great Temple with its ivory and cedar and gold. I thrilled to the throngs gathered for the morning sacrifice and to the smell of the offerings burning on the altar. This was the house of my God, to whom I felt a strange closeness. It was something I did not talk about, aware as I was that few of my companions understood or shared my feelings. No one born within sight of the Holy City, however, ever escaped its spell.

The terms of the treaty were relatively light— something which even at my age I found surprising until the necessity of haste on Nebuchadnezzar's part became known. Jehoiakim was to remain on the throne as a vassal of Babylon, and Judah was to pay an annual tribute. Nebuchadnezzar hoped that Jehoiakim, having tasted something of Babylonian power, would be a loyal vassal and that Judah would stand as a bulwark against Egypt where the Pharaoh was making ambitious moves toward the southwestern boundaries of the Babylonian confederacy. Though defeated by Nebuchadnezzar at the Battle of Carchemish a few months earlier, there was no surety against the Pharaoh's ambition to rule over an empire much wider than the boundaries of Egypt.

Within three days of the signing of the treaty, we were ready to depart. The tents were struck, the camels and asses were loaded, and Nebuchadnezzar with three companies of his soldiers and his few Jewish captives set out northeastward toward Babylon. The larger portion of the army was sent north to Tyre where trouble was anticipated.

The king and his personal staff, important officers, scribes, priests, and attendants traveled at a more rapid pace than the rest of the troop who were delayed by the slowness of the wagons and the beasts of burden as well as by the fact that the foot soldiers could not begin to keep up with the riders. With the foot soldiers came the rest of the exiles. This group of several thousand substantial citizens will, it is believed, make a considerable contribution to the financial welfare of Babylon since they are skilled in various trades, and there are priests and scholars among them. To see these families plucked up by the roots and transplanted into the midst of a pagan country is surely to witness a just punishment of God for the idolatry and paganism that had infiltrated Judah. It is, nevertheless, a sad thing to behold.

Mounted on horses from the stables of Jehoiakim, my three friends and I traveled generally in the vanguard of the king's company. The first day of the trip we learned the reason for Nebuchadnezzar's hasty departure. He had received word that the king, his father, had died suddenly, and he was hurrying home in order to establish his own authority and take a firm grip on the realm before his claims could be challenged or a revolt organized against him.

On that hasty journey I formed some strong friendships which would help to shape my life when I came to live in Babylon. Among the king's personal staff, without whom he never journeyed abroad, was the prince of the eunuchs. Nebuchadnezzar would let no one else supervise the preparation of his food. This important personage planned the menus and bargained with shepherds and farmers for their flocks and produce. He not only supervised the chefs, but he himself served the king and tasted his wines and dishes. Few men in the entire realm exercised more influence or had closer contacts with the king. His position was a strange one. He was not only the major domo to the royal household, but he was prince of all the eunuchs who served in the various offices in government as scribes, secretaries, and even judges and officers of the law. Ashpenaz—this was his name—was a rather portly man, taller than average, of a pleasant countenance dominated by beautiful sad eyes of a color I had never seen in a human face before—sort of an amber hue, they were, a shade you sometimes see in topaz quartz. Dignified in manner, he had none of the pomposity which I was to find so characteristic, generally, of the eunuchs I came to deal with in Babylon.

One of his ancestors, so I was told, had been a king of Nineveh. As a young boy he had been sent with his mother as a hostage to Babylon and there, while still a child, deprived of his manhood. This information made me uneasy, and I wondered if perhaps Nebuchadnezzar were planning for us a similar fate. There were, of course, eunuchs in the service of Jehoiakim, in whose presence I always felt uncomfortable; but Ashpenaz was different. Though I recognized something strange about him, it was not until the third day of the journey that I learned the nature of his physical state when it was mentioned quite casually by Belzephon, the son of the captain of the king's guard.

This young mounted bowman, barely a year older than I, was on his first military expedition. Brave in battle, he was shown no favors by his father and, because he never received nor expected special recognition, had become a favorite with many of the old veterans. He seemed to take more pride in his horse, a splendid stallion, than he did in his family heritage. With a handful of dates or raisins in our saddlebags and fresh, sweet water in our canteens, we loved to ride out ahead of the army, exploring the country through which we passed, investigating the ruins of old fortifications or ancient cities along the way. We would stop in the heat of the day in the shade of an outcropping of rocks or a row of scraggly trees to eat our lunch and rest an hour before heading back in the direction of the king's forces. Belzephon's light hunting bow could fell a bird on the wing even while Belzephon was riding at full gallop, and it was an unusual day that we did not bring back with us some wild game to the camp kitchen. Once Belzephon rode proudly into camp with a gazelle across his horse.

During the first few weeks of the journey, I tried to entice my Jewish companions to share the outings with us, but Hananiah and Mishael declared they wanted no more to do with the horse than was necessary and were quite content, after the initial soreness had subsided, to ride sedately with the king's forces. Azariah, on the other hand, who had taken to his horse with all the enthusiasm of a boy his age, would go along with us and soon became an expert, if somewhat reckless, rider.

We had little direct contact with Nebuchadnezzar. After the day's ride, he was busy with his secretaries and scribes reading the documents which were brought him by swift messenger from Babylon or occupied with the couriers' reports of affairs in other parts of the kingdom. Since we were traveling, for the most part, through territory that acknowledged the suzerainty of Babylon, the journey was a peaceful one. This was a well-traveled road, and we frequently passed caravans coming down from Arpad, Aleppo, or the kingdom of Lydia, far off to the northwest.

We interrupted the journey to rest for two nights at Damascus. The king and his immediate entourage were entertained in the citadel there, but the soldiers and the remainder of the troop camped outside the walls. From Damascus we began to travel in a more northeastward direction.

We turned more and more toward the east until we reached Tadmor, a magnificent city set in the midst of the desert in the most desolate part of Syria. Nebuchadnezzar was given a royal welcome, and we were entertained with lavish banquets and with due regard for his state. Again the major portion of the company remained in their tents outside the walls, but this time the four Hebrews were among those whom Nebuchadnezzar took with him into the city. We were fascinated by the wide avenues and the magnificent palaces, temples, and public buildings that lined both sides of the Street of Honor. Tadmor had been built on an oasis, and there were a number of splendid fountains. Though we were never able to discover the reason for it, Nebuchadnezzar demanded our attendance most of the time, and we had little opportunity to explore this attractive city or to have much contact with the people who lived there.

The architecture was strange to my eyes. The important buildings, some of great age, were erected of stone from quarries nearby and ornamented with carved tracery in fantastic designs of vines and flowers and fruit. Homes of the commoners were generally of brick made of sun-dried clay, which contrasted strangely with the magnificence of the temples of the gods and the palaces of the wealthy and important. Tadmor was approximately the halfway point of our journey and at the northernmost point of the curving route which we followed.

We began to head now in a southeastward direction. Captain Arioch told me that we were following roughly the course of the Euphrates, which lay far out of our sight beyond the horizon. At first there were no cities but quite a number of small villages, for this was now fertile farmland. Besides farmers, most of those whom we encountered on the road—if not royal couriers or merchant caravans—were nomadic people who regarded us with seeming indifference but moved from the road to give way for us while profanely struggling to keep their flocks and herds from scattering.

When we came within a few days' march of Babylon, we beheld great towers in the distance— huge mounds of brick of several levels with circling stairs or ramps leading up to some sort of building. I was told this building was usually a temple, though sometimes an observatory from which the priests and wise men observed the stars, attempting to learn from the planets the course of events still hidden in the womb of time.

Now we were coming to the end of the journey.

Nebuchadnezzar, entering Babylon for the first time as its ruler and sovereign, was determined to make as triumphal an appearance as possible. He chose, therefore, to enter by the great northern gate named for the goddess Ishtar. On either side great fortresses extended beyond the wall, and the roadway passed between them until it came to the outer wall itself. Later I was to find that this towering defense was wide enough for four horsemen to ride abreast along its top. Inside this wall there were two others almost as high, the three walls separated by open areas through which troops could move.

The city these walls enclosed was the largest in the world, encompassing a million and a quarter people and almost a day's journey on foot from east to west or north to south. As we approached the city, it seemed that these walls extended indefinitely on both sides of us. A short distance to our right was the River Euphrates, which we had crossed upstream the day before. Its waters flowed under the city walls and bisected Babylon dividing it into almost equal parts. The city had been built originally on what was almost the only high ground in the rich lowlands where the Tigris and the Euphrates, flowing closely side by side, would soon empty into the Gulf. A network of canals had been built to drain the areas near the city making it possible to control the spring floods. Small boats on these canals provided transportation for men and goods.

Along the Euphrates, both north and south of Babylon, were a number of smaller cities, each marked by a ziggurat. The territory between the two rivers was known—among other names—as Chaldea, and its inhabitants were known as Chaldeans; however, by the time of Nebuchadnezzar the word *Chaldeans* had taken on another meaning and was applied to the soothsayers and the wise men of the royal court.

Just inside the Ishtar Gate, we were met by the officials of the city—the governors, judges, satraps, priests, and eunuchs—who did full obeisance to Nebuchadnezzar as he marched between their prostrate ranks. An imposing figure in a skirt trimmed with fringe, and wearing a tall tiered hat and a goatskin draped over his shoulders, stepped forward and presented Nebuchadnezzar the crown of his late father, Nabopolassar. Later, Belzephon explained that this man was the acting high priest of Marduk, the chief deity of Babylon, the king himself holding the office of high priest to all the various gods. "Of course," Belzephon reported, "the king never does anything except appear in the high priest's vestments on ceremonial religious occasions."

Having received the symbol of royalty and still sitting astride his horse, Nebuchadnezzar raised the crown high and placed it on his head. The trumpets stationed along the walls on either side blared forth in triumph, and Nebuchadnezzar entered his capital as its unquestioned ruler.

The Ishtar Gate itself consisted of a high opening with heavy bronze doors in the outer wall. The three walls that encircled the city were joined on either side by walls of glazed brick gleaming in the sunlight. The bricks themselves were a brilliant blue adorned with yellow and white bulls and dragons in alternating rows one above the other.

Beyond the gates the processional road continued, ramping upward between high ornamental walls of the same blue enameled brick. These were adorned, however, with white lions, yellow-maned, and yellow lions with red manes, each higher than a tall man. Continuing along the stone-paved ceremonial way, we found that the walls, which had screened the king's palace on our right and a temple on our left, soon terminated and were replaced by the facade of public buildings, temples, and the homes of wealthy and noble Babylonians. Between them was open space given over to flower gardens and enclosed courtyards. We continued past a great ziggurat set in a wide plaza and arrived at the temple of Marduk. Entering the courtyard, we witnessed a sacrifice in thanksgiving for Nebuchadnezzar's victories and safe return to his royal city. To a good Jew the gods of the pagans are demons and idols. We found the king's worship most offensive but it was necessary for us, perforce, to remain until all was done.

Because of lack of space in the compound of the royal palace, my companions and I were housed in a building of three stories formerly used as a barracks for young officers-in-training. We were each assigned to a small, dark room with no window. Access to our quarters was through a curtained doorway that opened into a small inner court. We shared this building, known as the House of Princes, with some 200 other young men from all over the world. We recognized several nationalities as we passed to our quarters: Sidonians and Cypriots, Syrians from Damascus, soft-eyed Persians, as well as dark-skinned men from India and suntanned Ethiopians.

A few weeks after our arrival came six young men from Egypt, sons of Pharaoh or nobles of that land. As I listened to the variety of the languages in that house, I was reminded that we were in the city founded by Nimrod more than 1500 years earlier and shadowed by the Tower of Babel where God first confused the tongues of men. Each national group was assigned to the care and supervision and discipline of a eunuch. In fact, there were so many of these unfortunate creatures about the House of Princes that we used to refer to it jokingly as "the harem."

Our lives were busy and closely regulated. All

of us were put to learning Aramaic, the language of Babylon, as well as history, science, and mathematics, which I shall discuss in more detail later. Those who showed themselves lacking in skills and a willingness to apply themselves were weeded out. They simply disappeared. What happened to them we had no idea, although there were all sorts of rumors abroad that they were fed to Nebuchadnezzar's lions, were castrated, or were sent back to their homeland with brands on their foreheads. Fortunately, we Jews seemed to be doing well, though Mishael, Hananiah, and I had to keep after young Azariah who would daydream and found it difficult to apply himself to his studies. Of course, we were homesick, but we had little time to dwell upon it; so, to our surprise, almost three years passed quickly.

Contrary to the custom in Judea, the years of the king's reign are not numbered from the time he ascends the throne but from the beginning of the next year. What is described in Babylonian archives as the first year of Nebuchadnezzar's reign is actually the second year according to our Jewish reckoning. These years had not been without their problems, of course.

Almost from the beginning, we were faced with a major crisis. We had not been in Babylon more than a month before Melzar, the soft-hearted and genial eunuch who had been assigned to oversee us, instructed us to appear just after sunrise the next morning at the common room, which served as classroom and dining area for the four of us.

"This is the most important day of your lives," he began. "Even before you break your fast, I have been commanded by the prince of the eunuchs, Ashpenaz, to announce to you your Babylonian names." He paused and looked us over carefully one by one. "To you, Daniel, the prince of the eunuchs has assigned the name Belteshazzar. From henceforth, Hananiah shall be called Shadrach; and Mishael, Meshach. Now let us get down to the business at hand."

Pretending to ignore Azariah, who was his special favorite, he continued with instructions regarding our future schedule. Finally Azariah could contain himself no longer. "How about me, my lord? Don't I get a Babylonian name?"

"Oh, yes, did I forget to tell you? You are to be called Abednego." Melzar chuckled. "I am afraid these names are entirely too dignified and respectable for such rowdy young men. Meantime the prince of the eunuchs has bade me tell you that on the order of the king you are to address each other in public only by your Babylonian names and will speak generally in Aramaic, though you may use the language of the people with whom you have to deal in your administrative capacities."

"Now," he concluded, "you must put on these Babylonian garments, which will be your ordinary dress from this time forward."

As Judeans we were used to long and flowing garments. We found ourselves quickly at ease in the Babylonian costume, which consisted of a long-sleeved cotton shirt that reached to the ankles but was so fashioned that when the wearer walked the inside of the left leg was exposed to the middle of the thigh. Over this was worn a sleeveless cloak, open in the front and girded round with an elaborately embroidered sash of various colors. We found it a bit more difficult to become accustomed to the Babylonian headdress—which resembled one of the ziggurat towers—consisting of several circular sections, each slightly smaller than the one beneath it. However, for ordinary wear we were given a small dome-shaped cap, which we found quite comfortable except in the hottest weather.

A few days after we had donned our Babylonian garments and assumed our Babylonian names, Melzar, as one who brings good news, greeted us with an announcement: "Nebuchadnezzar, may he live forever, has appointed you all a portion of the king's meat and of the wine from the king's table. This means that you will be sent the finest foods enjoyed by the king himself, and nobody in Babylon will be better fed than will you and the others who dwell in the House of Princes."

He smiled upon each in turn; but when expressions of appreciation were not forthcoming, he said, "Are you not grateful for the king's bounty?"

Shadrach spoke first. "Melzar, perhaps you do not understand that Hebrews are governed by dietary laws. The king's table does not meet the requirements of those laws."

"But the king's steward procures the finest in

everything. All of the food is fresh and wholesome and served on dishes that are spotless and clean," Melzar protested.

"Yes," said Meshach, "but they are not ceremonially clean."

Abednego was already pointing out that certain meats are clean while others are regarded as unclean. "We cannot eat the kinds of fish that do not have scales or any meat that has not been drained of all its blood. Shellfish and pork are forbidden us."

I felt that the simplest way around this problem was to get an exception from Ashpenaz himself. I sent a request for permission to visit him, and, as I had known it would be, the prince of the eunuchs' reply was most gracious. The next day when I attended him in his quarters in the palace, he embraced me warmly and expressed his pleasure at my visit. After inquiring about his health and expressing hope that he had been able to get back down to the routine of his responsibilities in Babylon without too much of an adjustment and hoping that he was now over the tiresome journey which we had shared together, I explained to him our problem regarding the food from the king's table. I requested that, if possible, we be allowed a simpler diet.

He looked at me for a moment with his sad eyes of that strange color, got up from his chair, came over and put a hand on each of my shoulders, and, in disregard for royal command, addressed me by my Hebrew name as he had so many times on the long journey from Jerusalem.

"Daniel, somehow of all the men I have known, you are the one whom I would most like my firstborn son to have been were I able to beget children."

This was the first reference I had ever heard him make to his physical state.

"Perhaps your God has planted in my heart this affection which I feel for you, but the order that the princes are to be fed the same meat prepared for the king's palate came from Nebuchadnezzar himself. To disobey deliberately these high orders is to risk the loss of my head. You would not wish that, would you, my friend?"

I confessed that I would not wish to do anything to bring the slightest harm to one I had come to love and admire.

"Think of it this way. Is the difference between a smooth-skinned fish and a scaled fish important enough to die for? Is it worth risking the king's displeasure to prepare meats in milk gravy instead of serving them with wine sauce? Surely your God is reasonable enough to understand that when one becomes as you are now, a part of the king's household, you should follow the customs of that household."

No man could have been more gracious and at the same time more adamant in his refusal than was the royal steward, the prince of the eunuchs.

I remembered that down a small street— almost an alley—a short distance along the way to the House of Princes, was the dwelling of

Melzar. Wondering if at this hour of the day I could find him at home, I turned in that direction and was prepared to knock on the door of the courtyard when I found it unlatched and partially opened. As I entered, it creaked gently, waking Melzar who was nodding in the sunshine on a bench against the wall. He bade me welcome and clapped his hands to summon a slave whom he ordered to bring me a cup of fresh fruit juice; and in the sleepy stillness of that warm afternoon we sat and talked together.

Finally I said, "Would you like to make a wager?"

Immediately he was alert, and I had his full attention. Most Babylonians are as obsessed with games of chance as they are with necromancy and fortune-telling. Somehow these always seem to go together.

"But I thought you Jews did not believe in wagers."

"But this is a different matter," I replied. "Try us for ten days on the kind of diet we have lived on since we left Jerusalem. Nebuchadnezzar is very fond of lentils and soup made from onions and cucumbers. All Babylonians eat melons. What is wrong with these things? And give us mush and barley cakes. Let us have water to drink. Try it for ten days. I wager that at the end of that time, our faces and bodies will be as unmarked, our eyes as bright, and our breath as sweet as any in the House of Princes. If not, I will say no more about this matter."

"But you will be scrawny and sickly," protested Melzar.

"Are you sure now? Have we an undernourished appearance after that long journey on a simple diet? Let us make a game of this thing. Remember the king has said he will look upon us after three years. That is a long time off, and ten brief days are a small time to try our wager."

He sat in silence for a while, his eyes closed. Then he looked at me and smiled. "It is a poor wager that does not risk property or money, but I am risking the king's property and my life. You are, in a sense, wagering on the power of your God. I will agree. We will try it."

Exactly ten days later, my companions and I were in the warm bath in the House of Princes, a large and steamy room with pools and faucets and massage tables and bath attendants. There were, perhaps, some thirty or forty princes of other nationalities there at the time. In came Melzar looking us over very carefully, bidding us turn around so that he could see if there were any spots or pimples on our backs. He examined our ears (although I have no idea what he expected to find there), felt our muscles, and then turned his attention to other princes nearby, inspecting particularly the handsome Edomite lying on a slab while a slave massaged his back with perfumed oil.

"I must confess that my men are the best looking of the lot," he observed, proud as if he were the father of quadruplets.

For the next three years we continued on our

simple diet, refusing to defile ourselves with the unclean meats of the king's table or the sweet wines that he considered so healthy. During those three years there were times when sickness visited some of the princes. There were epidemics of various sorts, from mild distress to fatal illnesses. We heard that several young men died from a bloody flux; and others, in spite of the daily exercise to which we were assigned, became overweight and puffy. Others, wasted by weeks of dysentery, were hardly more than walking skeletons. Through it all, we Jews escaped untouched and unmarked.

At the end of three years, we were all, except Abednego, full-grown men; and he was taller and broader than any of us. Our hair was thick and wavy and our beards well grown. Our shoulders were wide, our muscles strong, and our bellies as flat as when we first arrived in Babylon.

Nebuchadnezzar was determined not only that his kingdom should be the largest and strongest the world had known, even exceeding the greatness of Nineveh so recently overthrown, but also that his capital should be the center of learning.

For the first few weeks our education had been almost entirely concentrated on learning to read the cuneiform writing, which consisted of wedge-shaped characters impressed upon clay tablets. We were assigned to read the *Enuma Elish,* which is the Babylonian account of creation, and from there we progressed to the *Epic of Gilgamesh*. Both books were to us poor perversions in many ways of the truth of God's revelation as set down by Moses. These works also served to introduce us to Chaldean theology and superstition, which, although based upon these ancient legends, have developed and changed over the centuries. Bel Marduk, for example, while worshipped as the creator of the world and the most important god in Babylon, was only slightly more popular with the common people than Nabu, better known as Nebo, who seemed to have been originally worshipped only in the town of Borsippa but had, for some reason, become a favorite of the citizens of Babylon.

The goddesses so important in the ancient legends had come to be less highly regarded. Although there were several of these female deities in the Chaldean pantheon, only one goddess really, Ishtar or Ashtoreth, was generally revered. She was now believed to embody the attributes of the other goddesses and was held in great reverence by those who sought her favor, since she was the goddess both of procreation and of war. It was thought that without her blessing there would be no continuation of life and no birth, either among men or the other creatures, and no fruit of the earth. A large order of her priestesses served as religious prostitutes, and her cult was one of lust and immorality. She was frequently referred to as the queen of heaven, and the crescent moon was her symbol.

The worship of Marduk and Ishtar dated from the first Babylonian empire, long before the rise of Nineveh. It is said that it was established by Nimrod himself from the founding of the city.

The priests, particularly those of the important deities, exercised a tremendous influence on the basis of their position as intercessors with the gods and as workers of magic, casting spells and performing incantations. Many of the astrologers were also priests and occupied high positions at court. No important governmental decisions could be made or policies established without consulting these oracles and soothsayers. Nebuchadnezzar required that the various cults maintain peace among themselves, and he insisted that the temples of all the gods enjoy the same privileges. But the truth is, there were terrific rivalries among the priests, who were always trying to stir up trouble to discredit those who served another deity. It was a rare occasion, however, when any of these soothsayers came before the king with conflicting advice or different interpretations of dreams or the movement of the heavenly bodies. They were much too clever for that. However much they disliked each other and however strong the jealousies between them, they were very careful to confer together and come to agreement before making their interpretations known to the king.

We next proceeded to the study of astronomy, and this necessitated many nights spent with our instructors at the top of a ziggurat learning about the motions of the heavenly bodies, since these were thought to affect closely the lives of men and nations and these cause-and-effect relationships were strongly emphasized. We studied the division of the stars, which were thought to move about the earth on three great pathways or roads. The astrologers themselves were divided on many points. We found, for example, that some were coming to believe that there should be a division of the heavenly bodies into twelve houses, each thirty degrees in length. The planets were named for the gods of Babylon as were the days of the week.

From astrology we progressed to the natural sciences, learning how to refine certain minerals by burning, and being taught to compound alloys. Mathematics was an essential part of our education since it was so necessary to the study of astronomy and the sciences and had practical applications in the measurements of squares and rectangles and in calculating the exact volume of a mass. We learned tables of squares, square roots, cubes, and cube roots. The Babylonians had inherited the sexagesimal system from the ancient Sumerians. (Their system of numbering was based upon sixties.)

While we were not expected to become physicians, unless we felt especially drawn to the subject and it pleased the king to let us major in that study, we learned some basic principles; but since illnesses were considered the work of demons or evil spirits, the spells cast by priests were more often resorted to than the rather elementary medical knowledge of the physician. Indeed, the two professions were so closely joined that most physicians were also priests. We had the opportunity to observe surgeons at work, and in this profession the Babylonians had considerable skill.

Nebuchadnezzar selected the wisest men he could find in each field of knowledge to be our instructors. Sometimes several men would be assigned to teach the same subject; and as could be expected when dealing with the so-called "exact sciences," there were many points of disagreement and a wide variety of conflicting theories expressed.

We were introduced to the esoteric arts of divination from the examination of the livers of animals and trained in the casting of spells, the readings of signs in nature, and in the exorcising of demons. Our Jewish upbringing and our faith in the God of heaven gave us discernment to detect truth from error. The words of the prophet Isaiah, set down a century before, purified our minds of the superstition and demonic influences so prevalent everywhere—except possibly in mathematics—in the "wisdom" of the Chaldeans.

Now, those who had persevered through three years of study were called to give an account of themselves before the king in the newly completed throne room of the palace, which had been under construction for as long as we had been students.

When he assumed the crown, Nebuchadnezzar took up residence in the palace that had been built by his father, Nabopolassar. One of the first acts of his reign was to begin construction of a new palace for himself on the great empty plaza just south of the royal residence. I sensed that he had this construction in mind for a long period of time, and I suspected that he had had architects and engineers working on the plans even while he was still the crown prince. The actual construction began within a month of his ascension to the throne and continued apace with architects, engineers, artisans, and craftsmen in such numbers that it seemed they would impede the work; but all went swiftly. Not a day passed, when Nebuchadnezzar was in Babylon, without his viewing the construction, issuing new commands, and changing something or other.

This great building was to cover approximately four times the area of Nabopolassar's palace and was in some places four stories high. Melzar told us that the gossip around the court was that when the new building was finished, Nebuchadnezzar intended to tear down his father's palace and use the area it had occupied to extend his own royal dwelling.

Nebuchadnezzar was a man obsessed with building and construction. Had he not been born to be king, he could have certainly been a successful architect. During his entire reign he spent almost every idle moment—and he had very few—seeking out new building materials and encouraging his overseers to devise new methods of brickmaking. When he visited Lebanon, he went into the mountains to inspect the tall cedar trees as they were being cut down and prepared for transport back to Babylon for use as ceiling beams. This earned him the nickname of "Woodcutter," although no one dared address him by that title.

As for the palace itself, it was much more than a monument to his pride or a satisfaction of his artistic nature. It was very necessary for an efficient government, for in addition to housing the king, his harem, and his servants and guards, it was to include the offices of the various departments of government now scattered here and there throughout the city, as well as quarters for envoys or visiting princes and their attendants.

Almost every year of his life, I was impressed with some hitherto unrecognized facet of this man's genius. Whatever he undertook, he did well. He was not only artistic, but he was also practical. He was not only of a creative temperament, but he was also a tremendous organizer and manager of men—a rare combination. He knew how to delegate authority and was a good judge of character, more often than not finding the right man for the place he was set to serve. He managed to keep himself in close touch with the most minute affairs of his kingdom and especially of his capital. Though his court was completely dominated by his personality and was quite Babylonian in its etiquette, he sought to make it cosmopolitan in character, as evidenced by his bringing young men like us from every corner of his widespread territories and beyond. Only a strong man, a tyrant by nature, could hold together a kingdom like this, made up of diverse people, speaking various tongues, and worshipping all kinds of gods; but this king could, on occasion, show himself surprisingly reasonable and fair in his judgments as he did on the occasion of our examination before him. I was impressed by the breadth of the king's knowledge and the skill with which he posed his questions. Some did not please him with their answers or manifest the quickness of wit which was to this king of such importance in those who served him.

The day following our meeting with Nebuchadnezzar, Melzar brought word to us that Ashpenaz, the prince of the eunuchs, desired our presence, and went with us to his quarters in the palace. Gracious as always, he greeted us as a man greets friends or as one who has good news he must share without delay.

"The king has informed me that among all those who stood before him yesterday, there was found none like the four princes of Judah."

Ever since I had arrived in Babylon, I had been conscious of strange stirrings about me, not sensed by my companions. I was like one who thinks he half sees a moving figure in the periphery of his vision and yet when he turns and looks directly, finds no one there.

From the time we left Jerusalem, we had not failed to observe all of the injunctions of our Jewish law, and, as far as possible in a heathen land, we sought to do all that was enjoined upon us in the commandments of our God. We never failed to pray at morning and evening toward Jerusalem and somehow among all the hours of our study found opportunity to read from the scrolls of the prophecy of Isaiah and the writings of Moses, which we had brought with us from Jerusalem.

I could not forget, even had I tried to do so, an experience that occurred on my first night within this great pagan city. Lying on my bed, I had what I thought was a dream but may have been a vision. I had hardly had enough experience thus far in these matters to distinguish between the two. I seemed to be again outside the city, approaching it as I had with Nebuchadnezzar's entourage. This time, however, instead of my seeing the city bright in the glory of the morning sunshine, it lay in shadows. No light was seen; no fires burned. Then I saw a lighted lamp brought into Babylon. The form of the bearer of the lamp I could not distinguish, for I beheld only his hand.

Suddenly all through the city there was a great wind blowing, swirling the formless, intangible clouds and darkness. It blew strong upon the lamp as if the force behind that tempest were determined to extinguish its light. But instead of blowing out the lamp, it scattered small sparks from the burning wick here and there. Many died out, but a few seemed to find a lamp to receive them, and they burned in their own places. Even from the dimmest of these flames, the darkness drew back and the dark cloud seemed to lift above where the flames shone. The vision—if it were such—faded away, or the dream ended, and left me lying wakeful on my couch in the darkness of my room in the House of Princes.

As I pondered what this could mean, a voice spoke clearly in the darkness: "The cloud you have seen suspended above this city is the judgment of God held back for a time. The veiling darkness is the sin and the evil, the harlotry and idolatry of this people; but I, the Lord, have brought you and your companions today as light into the darkness of this city. The winds of Sheol will seek to extinguish it, but the light of truth shall be scattered here and there and lodge in the hearts of some who hunger after righteousness. Fear not what evil men may do, for I, the God of heaven, have chosen you My servants, and My strength shall be in you. I have set over each of you an angel and have clothed you in the impregnable armor of My Spirit and My power."

I meditated upon this incident for several days before I told my companions about it. None had the slightest doubt that this was a message from God, and all were strengthened by it.

We sought to cultivate the friendship of the others quartered in this house with us, and some would come in the evening to question us about our homeland and the strange rumors they had heard about the religion of the Jews, who worshipped a God who had no form and of whom no image existed. Even Melzar, our mentor, a man more superstitious than religious and a strong believer in charms and magic, would sit in silence listening to us as we sang our Psalms together. We translated a few into Aramaic for his benefit, and eventually he joined the singing in a beautiful high voice.

One day a week we were free from our heavy schedule of studies and could do what we wished, and we chose the Sabbath as our rest day. There were a few Jewish families scattered throughout Babylon. A group of them lived together in a suburb some distance down the river south of Babylon, a community called Tel-Abib. When we had first arrived, some of these families called upon us ostensibly to welcome us to Babylon but really, I think, to learn the latest news from Jerusalem. They had invited us to visit in their homes, and we would very much have liked to spend the Sabbath with some of them; however, so extensive was the city of Babylon that none of them lived within a Sabbath's day journey of the House of Princes. Therefore, we had to observe the Sabbath rituals the best we could in our own quarters.

While we awaited our permanent assignments in the king's service, we were no longer required to live in the House of Princes. Many of those who had been in residence when we arrived were no longer there, having gone out to fulfill their assignments—many of them outside Babylon and others in parts of the city a considerable distance from the barracks, which were so far on the north side. Some could not wait to marry and had chosen homes for their wives and families. The king had granted us each a good allowance, and we had spent none of the funds which we had brought with us from Jerusalem. We decided, therefore, to find a house of our own and, after searching, rented a nice and roomy dwelling of two stories, built, as is the Babylonian fashion, around an open courtyard. It was very near the temple of Marduk, where I had been commanded to sit for the time being on an arbitration committee. The king, very wisely I thought, had established a committee of three men, none of whom worshipped any of the gods of Babylon, to settle disputes which were constantly arising among the priests of those gods. He felt that such a committee—all of whom, of course, were foreigners—would be more fair and impartial than any group of Babylonians. I hated my assignment but enjoyed tripping up the devious priests and exposing their deceits and lies.

Surely not since the days of Sodom and Gomorrah has there been a city like Babylon. Here lust is a way of life. Subtle violence and murder have become commonplace occurrences. All of this is the product not of the godlessness of the city, because much of it can be ascribed to the gods that are worshipped here. Men's basest desires are deified; there are gods who, in the opinion of their worshippers, will sanction any crime. There are in the city several hundred major temples to various gods—at least a half dozen of them to Marduk alone. Throughout this whole part of the kingdom are towers, temples, and shrines of all kinds.

The ziggurat, I am convinced, was created in this lowland where there are no mountains, as a substitute for the high places where man has always tended to set up his altars and plant groves where depravity and degeneracy are given free reign under the guise of worship of some demon god. Many orders of priestesses are, in fact, temple harlots; but there are a few exceptions, I am told. There is, however, much prostitution outside the temples, and one can hardly walk the street without being accosted quite brazenly and openly by a woman of that profession.

The slave market of Babylon is the largest in

the world—a great open square surrounded by a sort of cloister with pens where the unfortunate slaves are kept until they are brought out to the auction block, where men and women alike are displayed unclothed to the gaze of the buyers and the hundreds of depraved Babylonians who attend these auctions only for the purpose of gazing on naked human flesh.

It is rumored that there are some temples where poisons can be purchased secretly, and there is hardly any place of so-called "worship" where one cannot pay for a spell to be cast or a curse to be hurled against an enemy. I wonder if anyone knows accurately just how many gods are worshipped in this city—major gods of heaven, gods of earth and sea, important gods and goddesses, lesser gods and goddesses, spirits and demons.

Riches and squalor exist side by side in Babylon. The only paved avenue is the great processional way, which stretches from the Ishtar Gate across the city. This elevated avenue for processions, both royal and religious, is kept well swept and clean. The other streets—even the widest and busiest thoroughfares—are unpaved and littered with filth and garbage and in the rainy season are almost impassable for chariots or other vehicles. The garbage over the years can reach the point that it begins to cover the doors of the houses, in which case a new door is cut in the wall higher up with steps inside to lead down to the level of the courtyard.

The wealthy, the nobility, and the more important priests, in their houses with courtyards and terraces, live in great luxury, for the most part aloof from the stench of the city. The poorer classes—the craftsmen, the smaller merchants, and the lowest class of slaves—live surrounded by filth, both moral and physical.

When my people are allowed to return to Zion, I think it shall be with a proper hatred of paganism and idolatry, and I pray that they shall never again be tempted to go off after strange gods.

Our house was only a little farther from the palace where Meshach was advising the king's council on Jewish problems. Here he read and filed the reports from Jerusalem after writing out a summary of them to be taken to the king, who either dictated his own replies or instructed Meshach as to how he wished the replies to be handled. Generally, however, he left Meshach to make his own decisions, for he had quickly come to trust him.

As the interpreter and host for official guests, Shadrach spent most of the day at the palace or escorting visiting dignitaries around the city. Often when his duties required him to be present with these foreigners for banquets or special ceremonies until late in the evening, he slept in the palace where there was a room provided for him. Here he kept changes of garments so he could appear in fair and clean attire before the king the next morning, for Nebuchadnezzar was an early riser, eager to get down to the day's business. When not otherwise occupied, Shadrach was expected to be present whenever the king was holding court in the event an interpreter were needed. He seemed to enjoy not only the king's confidence, but his friendship also. Nebuchadnezzar always liked to be well briefed about those who came before him with petitions or with whom he was required to deal. Many a first-time visitor was surprised how much the king knew about him and how quickly he detected any inaccuracies in his statements, but Shadrach had bit by bit gathered that information in conversation with him or with those who accompanied him and briefed the king in advance of the audience.

Apparently Nebuchadnezzar was not sleeping well. Either he took his problems to bed with him, or his rich diet interfered with his rest. He complained of dreams, some of which came in fragments between snatches of sleep. The condition seemed to worsen toward the end of the year, and one morning he awoke even earlier than usual, irritable and troubled. While dressing, he gave command to summon all the wise men, fortune-tellers, and Chaldeans to his small audience chamber, a room which, in spite of its name, was as large as the throne room in Jehoiakim's palace at Jerusalem.

It was past noon before they could be brought together from the various parts of the city where they were busy with their incantations and spells in some temple or other or practicing their art for profit. An odd and unpleasant lot they were, some in tall pointed black hats, their dingy robes full of hidden pockets from which they brought out the objects the simple believed they plucked from thin air. There were red-garbed prognosticators, signs of the heavenly bodies upon them, others in strange, outlandish costumes which they felt lent to them an air of mystery, a few even with veils over their faces. With great gusto, they made their obeisances, troubled by this sudden summons but pretending to be wise and in full control of occult powers.

The dean of the Chaldeans, whose bright and evil eyes glinted craftily above a green-dyed beard so long he wore it tucked under his girdle, spoke in a voice surprisingly deep and beautiful in Accadian, the ancient language often used in rituals and religious ceremonies.

"O King, live forever. Tell your servants the dream, and we will certainly make clear the interpretation."

"I have forgotten the dream, and you will have to make known both the dream and the interpretation," the king replied with all the bluntness of which Aramaic is capable.

They could not have been more taken aback if he had hurled a thunderbolt among them. Noting the trembling and the consternation on the faces of all of the magicians and astrologers assembled there, Nebuchadnezzar grew more impatient by the moment. "You will either tell me the dream with the interpretation, or be cut in pieces and your houses turned into dunghills!"

Nergal-Zakiru, the head of the magicians, a tall, lank skeleton of a man with his skin drawn tightly over his bones, whined, "But, Your Majesty, there is not any man upon the earth who can tell you what you dreamed in the secret of your sleep. There is no king or ruler or lord that ever asked such a thing of any magician or astrologer or Chaldean. Only the gods know this, and their dwelling is not with flesh."

The king greatly disliked this trickster and had small confidence in him. "I know that you are not what you pretend to be. If I told you my dream, you could certainly make up some sort of interpretation—and I might have accepted it as true—but if you cannot tell me the dream, how can I trust you to devise the correct interpretation for it? Now you cannot provide lying and corrupt words. Tell me the dream, and I will know that you can show me the *correct* interpretation of it. If by this time tomorrow you do not satisfy me on this matter, you shall all be put to death, your families destroyed, and your houses leveled."

Arioch, the king's captain on duty that day, sensed what was coming, anticipating the worst. "Prepare tomorrow to kill off the lot of these rascals. Do not overlook one of the wise men or dealers in mysteries."

"O King, live forever," replied the captain. "You certainly do not mean this decree to apply to the princes you have brought together from all across the world and recently had trained in the knowledge of these mysteries."

"Every one of them!" bellowed Nebuchadnezzar. "They are all a pack of liars and deceivers!"

The frightened magicians, soothsayers, and Chaldeans made their groveling obeisances and a very hurried and ragged exit, one or two falling over as they backed out of the king's presence as etiquette required. Some were so frightened that they had to be half-carried by their companions.

As I was on my way home in the middle of the afternoon, wearied with all the priestly quarrels I had tried to arbitrate that day, Belzephon overtook me out of breath, excited, and frightened.

"King Nebuchadnezzar has ordered that all of the wise men—including soothsayers, Chaldeans, fortunetellers, and astrologers—shall be slain by noon tomorrow because they could not tell him what he dreamed!"

"Rest a moment, my friend, and get your breath," I urged, "and then you can start at the beginning and tell me the whole story as we go together to our house. But before you start with the story, how do you know all this?" I asked.

"Because my father has been commanded to organize this mass execution and is even now inquiring as to the whereabouts of all those who come under this sentence."

I did my best to calm my friend. "When we get home, we will talk this over quietly and decide what can be done. Then I will go with you to talk to your father and ask his advice."

We reached the house almost simultaneously with Shadrach, who, having been present at the king's court, could supply the details of the circumstances surrounding the king's rash and hurried condemnation of all the wise men of Babylon. Although Belzephon had informed me that we were all included in this sentence of the king, I felt sure he must be mistaken; but now Shadrach confirmed it. It was with considerable difficulty that I persuaded Belzephon to remain with Shadrach while I went to seek out Belzephon's father at the palace.

At the palace I found officials in confusion, and excitement running high. Some friends were bold enough to try to commiserate with me. Others, knowing I was one of those over whom was the shadow of death and the cloud of the king's displeasure, sought to avoid me. I found Arioch in the room assigned to the captain of the guard on duty. He greeted me, his face marked with concern.

"You heard of Nebuchadnezzar's orders that I am to take soldiers and destroy you and your friends together with all of the wise men of Babylon?"

"That is why I am here," I replied. "Why is the king in such haste to pass so extreme a sentence? Apparently, that dream must have been some terrible kind of nightmare to drive him to such frenzy."

I asked Arioch to get me an immediate audience with the king. "Come with me," he said. Taking me by the arm, he headed off in the direction of the king's quarters. As we walked along together, Arioch said, "As you know, it is proper etiquette to petition an audience and wait for permission before entering the king's presence, but in the mood he is in today, I half fancy he would refuse to talk to any of the wise men, including even you, Belteshazzar. We may be risking a further outburst of anger coming in like this unannounced, but, after all, I think you are a dead man already. As far as I am concerned, it is inconceivable that he will order me killed for bringing you before him like this."

As we passed from room to room, the soldiers on duty at the doors snapped to attention in the presence of their captain. At length, we came to the king's private chambers, and Arioch commanded the guards to open the doors. They followed his order without hesitation, and we found ourselves in the presence of Nebuchadnezzar. Again I felt that aura of power which had emanated from him the day I stood in the royal pavilion outside the walls of Jerusalem, but now it seemed to waver as with uncertainty.

Quickly I prostrated myself and remaining on my knees cried, "O King, live forever. I pray you forgive your servant for this sudden intrusion, but I have come to assure Your Majesty that if you will grant me time, I will show you the dream and the interpretation of it. The God whom I serve reveals the deep and secret things. He knows what is in the darkness, and light dwells with Him. He has given to me wisdom and might and will make known unto me this matter of concern to the king."

"How long will this take?" Nebuchadnezzar demanded.

"May it please the king, my God changes times and seasons, and wisdom and might are His;

however, He cannot be moved in His course nor hurried in His purpose. My companions and I will beseech Him if it be His will that He will graciously show me this thing tonight."

As I spoke those words before the king, there came to my mind in sudden remembrance the words that God had spoken to me my first night in Babylon. Somehow with that remembrance, I saw for the first time clearly the form of the angel of the Lord, not now barely discernible in the corner of my vision but standing between me and the angry king. An instant only I beheld him, but I knew he had not departed.

There was a change now in the king. I sensed his relief, like a man who, having made a too-hasty decision which he has come to regret, finds a way out of his dilemma.

"Let it be so then, Belteshazzar, but pray that your God reveals this mystery swiftly, for my dream—whatever it was—troubled me, for it seemed to be a revelation of things not yet accomplished but of great importance." He went so far as to express appreciation to Captain Arioch for bringing me so quickly to him and dismissed us almost graciously.

If Nebuchadnezzar felt a sense of relief, he was not alone. Arioch, sturdy and courageous soldier that he was, had no desire to slay unarmed men whose only guilt was their inability to tell a king what he had dreamed.

The shadows of evening were falling when I reached home. I found my friends waiting there with Belzephon, concerned for the news I brought. When they heard of my promise to the king to seek from the Lord the dream and its meaning, we agreed that we would eat no evening meal and spend the night in prayer desiring mercies of the God of heaven concerning this secret that we should not perish with the rest of the wise men of Babylon.

Belzephon said, "Let me stay here tonight and watch. I cannot pray to your God, for I am not His servant and He does not know me, but I would like to be here with you. I will remain, if you permit me, in this room while you go to your chambers and seek the face of your God."

"All things serve the purpose of our God. Babylon is like a golden cup in His hand; and though you may not know Him, He knows you. You can know Him. He welcomes all who come with earnest heart, asking His acceptance and trusting fully in His love and power to cleanse. But if you come, you must come knowing that He alone is God and renouncing the idols you have been brought up to worship and to fear," I told Belzephon.

Without a moment's hesitation, the young soldier replied, "Since I have been old enough to reason, I have known that these gods of stone and wood and precious metal were nothing but the creation of men's hands. I have no faith in them, nor do I fear their wrath; but since I came to know you, I have come to believe in your God who has no human form but who rules over the affairs of men, and my trust is in Him. Though I do not understand His law, nor am I taught in all of His commands, I claim Him as my God and shall seek to serve Him. I do not know how to pray to Him as you men pray, but I shall tonight seek His face while you bring this matter before Him."

We were all silent for a moment, Abednego openly weeping. I went to Belzephon and, embracing him, assured him that our God welcomed all who came in faith and that He turned no sincere soul away.

My companions gathered round this Babylonian to clasp his hands or embrace him, all of us rejoicing in this our first convert within the walls of Babylon.

The sky had grown darker with the descent of night, and the moon, which was now in its full phase, had not yet risen; so the shadows were thick in the room where we had not yet called for a servant to light the lamps.

Meshach said, "Go now, Daniel, to your room that the Lord may reveal this thing to you, but we will remain and pray here together with our new brother that the Lord shall be quick to reveal the secret that only the God of heaven knows."

In my chamber with the door closed, I spent the night, not on my bed but face down on the floor before the Lord. About midnight I became conscious of the fact that my room had grown lighter and that I could distinguish objects which the former darkness had obscured. The moon was now well above the horizon, its rays shining through the open window. A brightness flooded my mind and soul far stronger than the light of the moon. In a flash—a sudden revelation—I knew what Nebuchadnezzar had dreamed; and I poured out my heart in gratitude toward God, beseeching Him now to show me its meaning.

47

More slowly than the revelation of the dream had come, the interpretation was revealed. I blessed the God of heaven and gave Him praise, knowing that wisdom and might are His. As if I had never sensed the truth before, I became aware through the revelation of the dream how the God who changes the times and the seasons raises up kings and removes them. I felt myself drowned, as it were, in the wonder of His mercy and saw in Him the fount of all wisdom and knowledge which He is ready to impart to those who are possessed with a love for Him and a willingness to accept the revelation of His truth; He it is who sees in the darkness and brings wisdom to light, who is faithful unto His servants, and whose Word is forever unchanging.

Suddenly I was surprised to see that the night was gone, and the first rays of the rising sun were tinting with red and gold the sky above the palm trees in the garden. I washed and dressed myself quickly and hurried down the stairs to the room where Hananiah, Mishael, and Azariah were waiting with Belzephon. Somehow I could not in that moment think of them by their pagan Babylonian names; and it seemed only right that I should speak to them in Hebrew, but for Belzephon's sake, I began speaking Aramaic to tell them that our prayer was answered and God had revealed the secret of the king's matter, only to be interrupted by Hananiah.

"You do not need to tell us that, Daniel, for God has spoken to our hearts and told us that our prayers have been answered. Now let us eat. We have instructed a servant to set the table in the next room."

There, indeed, I found breakfast laid out by an early wakened servant who stood to serve us still half asleep. It was a simple meal of boiled eggs, olives, yogurt, and unleavened wafers washed down with fresh milk. I think I will always remember that meal—ordinary as it was—as the most delicious I have ever eaten. While we ate, no one questioned me about the revelation of the Lord. Our talk was all of His goodness and His grace.

Belzephon was like a new man. His countenance seemed to have changed. He moved as one with whom joy walks. He asked for explanation of passages he had heard us quote from the writings of Moses or Isaiah. The brave young warrior seemed no less brave but strangely tender. Meshach spoke of the vision or dream of the lamp and the sparks blown from its wick to light other lamps in the darkness of Babylon. Someone said, "This is the first of the lamps."

Belzephon insisted on walking with me to the palace to find his father. It was still early when we arrived, but Arioch had obviously spent the night in the king's house. His armor and helmet were polished, and his cape was fresh and well pressed. He looked at his son strangely for a moment as if about to inquire what he was doing here with me but seemed to change his mind, urging me to make haste to go with him to the king.

This time we were taken straight to the king's bedroom where we found him still in his nightdress. Arioch said, choosing his words very strangely I thought, "I brought you a man of the captives of Judah that will make known unto the king the interpretation."

Nebuchadnezzar reached out and took me by the arm. "Are you able to make known unto me the dream and the interpretation?"

I bowed my head in acknowledgment replying, "The secret which the king demanded that the wise men, the astrologers, the magicians, and the soothsayers show to the king they could not show; but there is a God in heaven who reveals secrets, and He it is who makes known to King Nebuchadnezzar what shall come to pass in the last days. Here is the dream and the vision that came to you upon your bed. It is the God who reveals secrets who makes the future known to the king, but the secret has not been revealed to me because of any wisdom that I have more than any other man but for the sakes of those who are able to make known interpretations to the king and help you understand the thoughts of your own heart."

I made this introduction before beginning to show the revelation, for I wanted Nebuchadnezzar to understand clearly that it was the God of heaven who had condescended to share with him, a mere man, the secrets of those things which would come to pass in the last days.

"Here is your dream. You beheld a great image of extreme brightness and terrible form. The head of the image was of fine gold, the breast and the arms were of silver, and the belly and the loins were of brass. His legs were made of iron, and his feet were partly iron and partly clay. You beheld the image until a stone, not cut out by human hands, smote the image upon his feet that were of iron and clay, and they broke to pieces. But that was not all. The brass, the silver, and the gold broke to pieces together with the iron and clay and became mere chaff on the threshing floors in the summertime; and as the chaff is carried away, so the wind carried all of the fragments of the image away, and they were not found. But the stone that smote the image became a great mountain and filled the whole earth. This was your dream, was it not?"

The king slowly nodded his head. "And the interpretation?"

"This is it, O Nebuchadnezzar. You are a king of kings because the God of heaven has given you a kingdom and the power and the strength and the glory. Wherever men dwell, the beasts of the field and the fowls of heaven He has given into your hand, and He has made you ruler over them all. You are the head of gold."

The king sat silent listening as one entranced.

"But after you are gone, another kingdom shall rise, inferior to yours. Then shall come a third kingdom of brass, which shall take over the rule of the earth. The fourth kingdom shall be as strong as iron, because iron breaks in pieces and subdues everything; so it shall break in pieces and bruise."

When I had begun to reveal to the king that one day his kingdom should be taken over by another, and that by another, he came to his feet and began slowly walking up and down the chamber, listening intently and concentrating upon the revelation.

"And as you saw in the toes iron and clay mixed together, so those latter kingdoms shall be a mixture of the various races and people, but they will not be united with each other, even as iron cannot be mixed with clay. In the days of these kings, one God who rules in heaven shall set up His kingdom; it shall never be destroyed or left to other people, but instead it will break in pieces and absorb all of these other kingdoms and shall stand forever."

Now Nebuchadnezzar had ceased his pacing up and down across the tiled floor. Like one exhausted from a long journey, he slowly sank to cushions thrown on the floor near the place where I stood.

"And what of the stone I saw cut out of the mountain without hands?" his voice was scarcely audible.

"You saw that it broke the iron, the brass, the clay, the silver, and the gold; and in this dream the great God has made known to the king what shall come to pass in the great and final kingdom of the earth. The dream is a true revelation of God's plan, and the interpretation I have given you is certain and accurate and genuine."

Nebuchadnezzar half rose from the cushions to

prostrate himself before me, touching his forehead to my feet. Embarrassed to see this great king so humiliate himself and fearing that later, having thought upon it, he would be alienated from me by embarrassment, I did that which is forbidden. I touched the king's person, stooped and sought to take him by the shoulders and the arms and lift him to his feet. All this time, Arioch had not moved. Nebuchadnezzar, who until this moment had seemingly forgotten his presence, now commanded him to go and call in the officers of the court and the royal chamberlain who were waiting in the small audience chamber for the king to make his appearance.

Arioch bowed, backed toward the door moving stiffly like a man who has been too long in the cold, threw open the two valves of the door and cried in a loud voice, "The king commands the presence of all of you."

He stood aside as they entered the room, perhaps thirty altogether: my friend, Ashpenaz, the royal steward; officers of the court; cunuchs; and a few ambassadors who had arrived early for their appointments with the king. Notably absent were the wise men, the soothsayers, the astrologers, and all of the other interpreters of dreams.

The king gave command that they should offer an oblation and anoint me with sweet ointments. Feeling strange and wishing I were anywhere else but here, I waited until they came with the incense and the perfumed oils. My heart rejoiced as the king said to me, "It is true that your God is a God of gods and a ruler of kings and a revealer of secrets. He has shown this by enabling you to reveal this secret."

All of those in the room, except the king, who had risen to his feet, were now on their faces before me. The king called for the scribes to stand. "Let it be known through all parts of my realm that I declare Daniel to be a great man, and I have made him to be ruler over the whole province of Babylon. He is to be the chief of the governors over all of the wise men of Babylon."

He then commanded that gifts be brought from the treasury, and he assigned to me slaves who could bear the treasure and who were skilled in cooking and household chores. He commanded the lawyers to draw up a deed and register it making me the owner of a large house—a small palace, really—that he had recently confiscated from its owner, a nobleman found guilty of treason and put to death. All of this was done over my protest, for I had no ambition for power or riches except as they might enable me to serve more effectively the God of heaven.

When all this was done, Nebuchadnezzar inquired if there were anything else that I desired. I replied, "Great King, I deserve no rewards. I have done only that which was my duty, and I am grateful to my God that I have been able to show the king his dream and the interpretation of it; but since you have so graciously bestowed upon me riches and honor and power, you have also placed responsibilities upon my shoulders of which I am not only unworthy but hardly able to bear. If it would please the king to set Shadrach, Meshach, and Abednego over the affairs of the province of Babylon, it would make my burden lighter and they will be as faithful in their service to the king as I have tried to be."

Without hesitation, Nebuchadnezzar ordered it done, making them answerable only to me.

One would think that the necromancers, fortune tellers, soothsayers, and Chaldeans would have been grateful for the fact that God had made it possible for me to reveal the king's dream and the interpretation of it and thus spare their lives and save their families. Some few were, but, human nature being what it is, I think I made more enemies than friends because of this thing. Some underhandedly spun their plots and wove their webs in an effort to harass and burden me further and turn the king's favor from me. Others, who had been close to Nebuchadnezzar and found his ear open to their petitions, were now on a different basis. Having lost the king's confidence, they lost his favor as well; and as my position and power increased, so theirs declined. As the governor, I held the power of life and death over them, but I chose, except in those cases where their scheming offered some slight threat to the peace of the city or some offense or rebellion against Nebuchadnezzar, to ignore them or merely banish them from the city for a while. But I had good cause daily to thank God for the gift of the discerning of spirits which enabled me to know their minds and hearts and see their evil designs long before they could actually be put into practice.

Knowing that a king's favor carries with it threats and dangers from the disaffected and the jealous, Nebuchadnezzar said to me one day, "You need your own bodyguard, a small troop of men to guard you and protect your house. Is there anyone in the army whom you would particularly like to have as the captain of the troop?"

"Of all the soldiers I know, none is more faithful a man than Belzephon, the young archer and the son of Captain Arioch. If you could spare him, I would count it the greatest joy to have him not only as a bodyguard but also as a friend, especially now that Meshach, Shadrach, and Abednego each has his own house and I see them all too infrequently. He is, however, a man who can make a great name and fortune for himself as an officer in the king's armies, and I feel I am selfish to ask that so talented and mighty an officer be given the little task and small responsibility of protecting the king's servant. Besides this, I have the promise of the God of heaven that no harm can befall me as long as I live in Babylon; and I really have no need of bodyguards since there is a heavenly warrior who protects me."

The king remained thoughtful for a moment. "Belteshazzar, if all the angels which serve your God in heaven were sent to protect you, no one in Babylon, from the king to the poorest beggar, could catch sight of them. Your position is one that commands respect, and there is nothing people respect more than a show of power and pomp. For that reason, if for no other, you shall have Belzephon as your chief bodyguard and the commander of the soldiers who guard your house and make way for you when you pass through the crowded streets."

When Belzephon heard of his new appointment, he came to me immediately saying, "My brother, the God of heaven whom I trust has answered my prayers." He proceeded to tell me that from this time forward he was assigned to guard and protect me. I was moved, of course, by this enthusiastic acceptance of the king's assignment.

"You mean, my friend, that you asked God that you, a young officer and a man with perhaps a great future in the armies of Babylon, could be assigned to this small position?"

"To be the commander in chief of Nebuchadnezzar's armies would not be half the privilege the king has bestowed upon me. I need to know more of the law of our God and be taught His ways. In your household, I can eat those things which He commands and, like you, keep myself undefiled from the things which He forbids. There are a thousand temptations for a young officer in the city of Babylon—in its inns and taverns—that I shall not face in this household." He smiled widely for a moment. "Besides, I never did succeed in teaching you to put an arrow in a target; and maybe as busy as you are now, we can find an occasional afternoon to ride out hunting, and I may make a good bowman of you yet."

Nebuchadnezzar was always very careful to observe all of the important ceremonies attendant upon the worship of the temples, but the most important was the Akitu Festival observed each year to celebrate the new year which fell, according to the Babylonian calendar, between the first and twelfth of the month Nisanu, which we call in the Hebrew "Nisan." The rite was a reenactment of their idea of the creation of the world. The ceremony was at the same time as the renewal of the king's right to reign. The myth of creation was enacted in full twice during the Festival. After the first enactment, the king was ceremonially deposed and went before the shrine of Marduk in his temple to confess his sins. A selected priest, masked so that the king could not recognize him, slapped the king until the tears ran, this being interpreted as a sign of Marduk's favor. The king then took the hands of the god and pledged himself to serve the powers of heaven faithfully.

Immediately following this ceremony, a condemned prisoner was led in disgrace through the streets. At the Ishtar Gate, the sins of the city were ceremonially laid upon him, and he was driven out with whips and stones to banishment; thus, according to Babylonian belief, were the citizens freed of guilt and prepared to enjoy the favor of the gods for another year.

Meantime, the "Woodcutter" continued his building program, leveling whole sections of the city which he felt were run down and a blot upon the beauty of great Babylon, replacing them with new construction bisected by straight streets parallel to the river or at right angles to it. Outside the city, construction went on apace. The suburb of Tel-Abib, located near the juncture of the canal called Chebar and the Euphrates, was enlarged by further filling in the marshy land around it, and new houses of dried brick were built upon this filled land. The canals were silting up with the mud brought down by the Tigris but more so by the washing away of their banks. The king determined to put a stop to this and lined the banks of the canal with bricks, kiln-dried and glazed and set in bitumen as mortar, to retain the mud through which the canals were cut.

He repaired and redecorated the temples, giving particular attention to those of some of the minor deities whose priests were complaining that the edifices of their gods were being allowed to decay or fall into disrepair while those of the more important deities were being embellished, adorned, and enriched.

All of this construction required a tremendous

amount of clay for the making of brick. The areas outside the wall from which this clay was taken were filled with water from the rivers, providing a moat surrounding the city on all sides and affording additional protection against an invasion. New kilns were built, and new glazes were perfected. When houses were built of unglazed, sun-dried brick, the outside wall was often hardened by building a fire along its base, thus further hardening the clay; but on all important buildings, the outside layers of brick were always glazed to an enamel-like brilliance providing both strength and beauty to the construction.

I was troubled by news from the West where the Pharaoh was enticing my royal uncle by flattery and promises of his protection to cast off his allegiance to Babylon and withhold his tribute. Although Nebuchadnezzar preferred building to fighting, matters came to such a pass that he found it necessary to embark on a military expedition to deal with Judah.

It is a mark of Nebuchadnezzar's trust in me that he did not remove me from my position as what amounted to the regent of the city in his absence, but he did suggest that I keep a careful eye upon the Jews of Babylon in case "they might hear rumors" that he was attacking Jerusalem. The army that left the city toward the beginning of winter in the month of Kislimu, late in the seventh year of Nebuchadnezzar's reign, was well equipped, well trained, and well prepared.

Evidently Nebuchadnezzar made a forced march, or the siege of Jerusalem was brief, because it was almost exactly a year later that word reached us of the fall of Judah's capital. My uncle Jehoiakim had died some three and a half months before the fall of the city, and Jehoiachin had succeeded to the throne. I could take some degree of comfort from the fact that my uncle Jehoiakim had not fallen into the hands of Nebuchadnezzar who, indeed, had every right to be in a vengeful mood against him, for in spite of the warnings of the prophet Jeremiah, Jehoiakim had indeed made common cause with the Pharaoh of Egypt and had finally cut off altogether the tribute promised to Nebuchadnezzar.

This time the Babylonian king was not gentle. He brought back to Babylon with him the gold and silver vessels of the Temple; the eighteen-year-old King Jehoiachin and his mother, Queen Nehushta; leading officials; and particularly the ironworkers and skilled craftsmen. He did not, however, destroy Jerusalem or burn and level the city but placed Zedekiah, another relative of mine, on the throne as his vassal.

Though, perforce, maintaining calm faces in public when the news of the fall of the city was received, I and my comrades of the tribe of Judah mourned in the privacy of our homes. Each dispatch from Judah was like another arrow piercing our flesh. The heaviest blow of all, however, came with the news of the defilement of the Temple and the desecration of the sacred vessels of our God.

It was some months before the bedraggled captives reached Babylon. Most of the Jews were assigned to live in Tel-Abib and a few other suburbs. Jehoiachin and his family were placed in great poverty under a sort of house arrest and were not allowed to forget that they were prisoners of Babylon's king.

Among the captives was Ezekiel, a man to whom God spoke, a prophet and a seer of the future to the very end of time. Unfortunately, I saw him all too seldom, settled as he was among the captives on the banks of the Chebar not far from Tel-Abib. His visions and the word of his prophecy are set down in the Book which he wrote under the inspiration of the divine Spirit. He was sent of God to comfort and bless the Jews in exile as I was given primarily to declare the Word of the Lord to Babylon and its ruler. He is a few years older than I and a member of the priestly tribe. I think it is because of his scholarship and reputation for piety that they included him with those taken into captivity.

I am glad that Jeremiah was left in the homeland. I think my real love for God is due to Jeremiah's influence upon me when I was young. He loves the Covenant people; but, more, he loves the God of the Covenant. A very serious man who rarely smiles and whom I never heard laugh, he does not have the personal charm of Ezekiel. I am afraid that his ministry in these years ahead will be one of tremendous sacrifice and emotional suffering. He has already endured the mockery and persecution with which God's servants are so often afflicted.

Within a few months of his return to his capital, Nebuchadnezzar appointed Nabonidus, his son-in-law, the governor of Babylon. It was a more or less honorary appointment, for I continued to exercise the authority the king had granted me as governor of the province of Babylon, which included a large area surrounding the city. It was plain that he felt uncomfortable with me, perhaps feeling that I might be bitter and no longer fully to be trusted because of his dealings with Jerusalem and particularly the desecration of the Temple of my God. It was now that he began to employ me occasionally as a foreign ambassador or on business at a considerable distance from the city itself.

In the next few years a great many changes took place in my own household, and not the least of these affected Belzephon. By faith, he was a Jewish proselyte and, as such, should be circumcised. There were now Jewish priests in Babylon, brought here among Nebuchadnezzar's captives. We arranged for one of these priests to perform the ceremony at my house knowing that should Belzephon make the trip to Tel-Abib for the ceremony he would be too sore and uncomfortable to return with us. As it was, he had a very uncomfortable few days during which he could not endure any garment upon him and remained in his own room where his food was brought to him.

The priest who performed the rite, Elhaman by name, was one of those rare men to whom the law of God was precious, and his very presence brought a blessing to our hearts. I invited him to dinner, and it was not long until he became a frequent and most welcome visitor. He had not yet recovered from the loss of his wife, who had died on the journey from Jerusalem to Babylon, heartbroken by the fall of the city and the desecration of the Temple; but his two daughters, named for the wives of Jacob, Leah and Rachel, would sometimes join their father. Leah was at eighteen a striking beauty with hair that shone reddish-brown in the sunlight and strange green eyes that sparkled with humor and which I surmised could burn with rage and anger also. Quick-tongued, she handled the Hebrew language like a rapier; and as Abednego once remarked, "When she becomes proficient in Aramaic, she will have a dagger in each hand."

Rachel, her twin, had skin as fair as her sister's, but her hair was darker and without the reddish glints. Her voice was soft and gentle, and her limpid, dark eyes more often downcast than meeting the gaze of men. She was, her father declared, like her late mother—thoughtful and kind. Her speech did not often strike sparks like her sister's but seemed to assuage like perfumed ointment the ruffled spirits of her hearers.

Belzephon could not take his eyes off Rachel, and I noticed that Abednego always managed to be present when Leah was visiting.

My cousin Jehoiachin and his mother were living in a small house somewhat apart from the rest of the exiles near Tel-Abib. Because his father, my uncle Jehoiakim, had set him such a poor example of piety and because of the wickedness of his mother, Jehoiachin had little respect for the religion of his fathers. Nonetheless, he was regarded by the exiles who had been carried captive with him to Babylon, as well as the great mass of the remnant left behind in Judah, as their lawful king. Zedekiah, a twenty-year-old whom Nebuchadnezzar had placed upon the throne of Jerusalem as a vassal of Babylon, was, according to the reports that came to us, doing that which was evil in the sight of the Lord and refusing to hearken to the prophet Jeremiah, who was at that time the voice of God in Judah. It seemed plain to me—whether this came by divine revelation or from knowledge and experience—that the time was close at hand when Nebuchadnezzar would level Jerusalem and put an end to the kingdom of Judah.

I felt, however, an obligation to my aunt, ungodly as she was. When I was a boy, she had always treated me with kindness if not with affection; therefore, I went to visit her, taking with me some things I felt she would have need of but not gifts rich enough to arouse the anger of the king or lead him to suspect that I was conspiring with his royal prisoners. I found her much aged since I had seen her last, and the great pride which had been such a noticeable part of her temperament had turned to bitterness as wine sours into vinegar. Before I was taken to Babylon, my cousin Jehoiachin had struck me as a spoiled brat who, unless some miracle intervened, would grow up to be a dissolute and ungodly man as, indeed, he had.

I mention this visit because it was here in the midst of a colony of captive people that I met for the first time Nebuchadnezzar's favorite wife and queen, Amytis. The daughter of Cyaxares, king of the Medes, she had been given in marriage to Nebuchadnezzar to seal the alliance between Media and Babylon. Though the king preferred her above all women, and apparently she was devoted to Nebuchadnezzar, she could not get over the feeling—even after all these years—that she was a stranger and an alien in a foreign country. Perhaps it was this that prompted her desire to meet the exiled queen of Judah.

Amytis had recently recovered from an illness which the physicians suspected was the result of homesickness for Media with its high terrain, its mountains, and its forests; and Nebuchadnezzar, therefore, did not feel he could refuse her permission to call on the erstwhile queen of the Jews, insisting only that the visit be as inconspicuous as possible. She, therefore, had come directly from the palace on an unmarked barge down the Euphrates accompanied by only the boatmen, a eunuch as bodyguard, and one lady of the court.

Unaware of Amytis's plans to visit my aunt, I happened to choose the same time to call upon her. Belzephon, who the king insisted should accompany me everywhere, came with me by hired boat down the river, each of us plainly dressed and with nothing to distinguish us as either the official or the officer.

Here in this country suburb, the modest houses

were not crowded together as in the city but set in vegetable patches with pigeon houses and stables. When we approached the nondescript house of my aunt and my cousin, I recognized the eunuch, Migir-Nebo, who was keeping watch at the door. For a moment I was puzzled by his presence here but then realized that Queen Amytis must be inside. He did not at first recognize us without our formal garments and stood threateningly in our way. Belzephon, resenting this affront to my dignity, stepped forward to confront the eunuch. I laid a hand on his arm, however, and, calling the queen's guard by name, assured him that if Queen Amytis were visiting here, we would wait outside until she left, as we had no wish to intrude upon the queen. The eunuch, upon hearing my voice, fell on his face pouring forth apologies as a drainspout pours out water on a rainy day.

At this juncture, a sallow young man appeared in the doorway demanding to know who I was and what the noise was all about. Before I could speak, the frightened eunuch answered, "This is the wisest man in Babylon and the favorite of King Nebuchadnezzar, may he live forever. Bow down and do obeisance to the governor of the province of Babylon."

"Just a moment," I interjected. "Unless I am wrong in my speculation, you are Jehoiachin, formerly and for a short time king of Judah, are you not?"

"I am Jehoiachin, still king of Judah, though brought here in chains and humiliation as a captive by this same Nebuchadnezzar."

I took a step toward the door as the eunuch backed off to one side, and Belzephon moved up to stand shoulder to shoulder with me.

"Cousin, you had better learn some manners before King Nebuchadnezzar, may he live forever, has you skinned alive and your hide nailed to the wall of his palace."

Jehoiachin, not the least cowed but turning red with anger, said, "How dare you call the king of Israel 'cousin'! I am no cousin of yours!"

"I assure you," I said, "that I am not proud of the relationship, but I am, whether either of us likes it or not, your cousin. When I lived in the palace of your father and knew you as a child, my name was Daniel."

It was plain from the pallor of his face that he had heard how Daniel, the friend of the great king, was now a man set over the affairs of Babylon. He was plainly taken aback that this plainly dressed stranger could be a man of such importance. He evidently thought my threat, uttered in jest, might be carried out, for turning he called over his shoulder, "Mother, here is your nephew Daniel. Come quickly and greet him."

This entire encounter had evidently been overheard within the house, for not one queen came out but two. Belzephon and I first made our obeisance to Queen Amytis, and then turning to my aunt, I presented to her the captain of my guard.

"And is he not to be presented to me?" asked

Amytis.

"I crave your pardon, my queen, for this seeming rudeness. I took it for granted because his father is the captain of Nebuchadnezzar's guard and one of the most distinguished officers in his army that this noble son of his has had the privilege of being presented to you before."

I was relieved to see what was definitely a twinkle in the eyes of the queen of Babylon.

"Is it so strange that in the midst of court etiquette I have never met this young man, since until this moment I have never laid eyes on Belteshazzar, the most famous man—after the king, of course—in all of Chaldea?"

After we had chatted for a few moments standing there in that tiny, weed-grown courtyard, I prepared to withdraw, explaining that I had no wish to intrude upon the visit of Queen Amytis to my aunt and that I had come only to inquire after her welfare and that of my cousin. I presented my simple gifts, requesting that Nehushta feel free to call upon me at any time I could serve her.

Queen Amytis signaled for her attendant lady and the eunuch to prepare to go. "I was just on the point of returning to the palace. I would like for you, wise man, and you, noble warrior, to attend me in my barge."

This, of course, amounted to a royal command, and there was nothing we could do but acquiesce with thanks. I was, however, delighted to have this opportunity to get to know this queen, so sad and homesick in the midst of so much luxury and power. The longer I was in her presence, the more I was impressed with her gracious, natural manner and the sense of humor so near the surface but too often hidden beneath her melancholy spirits.

As we sat in the bow of the barge a little apart from the others, she surprised me by saying, "I know of your regard for the king, my husband, and of your loyalty to him. Even though you are, in a sense, a captive, you do not have the attitude of an alien and a man compelled to serve by reason of circumstances which may seem to you unfortunate."

I bowed my head in acknowledgment but did not reply.

"The king is often uneasy in mind, and I have heard how your interpretation of his dream brought quiet for a while to his troubled soul. I sense also a strange aura about you, as of one whom the gods have chosen, if, indeed, the gods exist. Will you come to the palace sometime and talk to me about this invisible God of yours? For if a God there be, then surely He does not enter into the idols that men carve nor dwell in a hundred temples scattered throughout our kingdom."

I assured the queen that I was entirely at her service, and that in nothing was I more honored than in the queen's request to come and tell her of the God of heaven.

What she said to Nebuchadnezzar about this brief encounter, I never learned, but the next time

I was in his presence, he signaled me to remain when he dismissed his court.

"Belteshazzar, Queen Amytis has told me about the chance meeting she had with you, and I find her somewhat recovered from her melancholy. I would like for you to present yourself before her at her request and act as her counselor. You are one man I know can be trusted to treat the queen with all dignity and due respect."

I thanked the king for his confidence and assured him of my willingness to serve him and his queen in any way it pleased them to command me.

"O King, live forever, may I make bold to offer a suggestion which I think will cheer the heart of the queen and at the same time give to you, who love the art of building, great pleasure?"

At the mention of his love for building, he looked up from the winecup in his hand, his interest captured.

"Could you not have your architects, in the area where your father's palace stood, erect a house that is like a mountain and a huge pavilion that will remind the queen of her homeland? Your engineers who can build great ziggurats could fashion an edifice of this sort, wherein exotic birds could sing and strange animals find a home among trees and flowers native to Queen Amytis's homeland. Surely nothing could more cheer her heart or drive away the sadness of her spirit."

Another man, even a king as rich as Nebuchadnezzar, might have said, "Have you taken account of the cost of such a project?" or found some other excuse for turning so presumptuous a suggestion aside, but not Nebuchadnezzar. It was obvious that the idea had struck a spark of interest in his mind; so without hesitation, he thanked me for the suggestion and promised to give it consideration.

 The next day the king commanded my presence. "I have been thinking, Belteshazzar, of your suggestion about erecting a building like a mountain against the sky. In fact, I lay awake most of the night turning over in my mind how such a thing could be done. My best architects and engineers are at this time south of Ur rebuilding the docks and seawalls at the north end of the gulf and remodeling two of the temples there that have fallen into disrepair. Discuss this matter with them. Work on some sketches and possible plans, and bring them back here to me. If, however, you think they are practical and workable, command Nebo-tsabit, the chief architect, to bring two of his best engineers and return with you to Babylon, leaving the work at Eridu in the hands of his assistant architects and the rest of the engineers." I assured the king that I would leave first thing the next morning and went to my house to prepare for the journey.

In the hot and humid climate of Babylon and the delta region below it, a journey down the river would be a pleasant relaxation, especially as we drew near the gulf and a possible sea breeze. The concern of Nebuchadnezzar for the welfare of his entire kingdom was evidenced by the floodwalls constructed here and there where the banks of the river were low and by the new docks and warehouses which lined those banks at frequent intervals, turning the very river itself into a port and harbor where the largest vessels could unload their cargos.

We spent a night at Ur, giving the boatmen a very welcome rest. My Jewish heart thrilled at walking the streets of that most ancient city, the home of our father Abraham, from whence he was called to go forth to the land which God had chosen to give to him and his descendants. Even in Abraham's time, Ur had been dominated by the worship of the moon goddess who, though her name had been changed somewhere down the centuries, was now identified in this city as Ashtoreth. In spite of all the time and money Nebuchadnezzar had spent upon the city, Ur still gave the impression of a provincial town with no paved ceremonial way and with houses built, for the most part, only of sun-dried brick, constantly in need of repair because of the rainstorms and occasional springtime floods which inundated the low-lying town.

Eridu, though it had declined as a commercial port since the building of the docks farther up the river, was still of considerable importance as the home port of the Babylonian navy. Enamored as he was with construction of all sorts, Nebuchadnezzar had established large shipyards here for the building of vessels of war. He had sought to train a navy and had hired experienced sea captains from anywhere he could find them. Perhaps because the king himself was not a seagoing man or fond of the ocean, the encounters of his navy were seldom mentioned in the archives and little talked about in the streets of the capital.

Accompanied by Belzephon and two of his soldiers and a small retinue of scribes and slaves to impress upon the king's architects and engineers the importance of my visit, we found them at the temple of Enki, which was undergoing repairs. Enki was the most honored god in this area since it was believed he controlled the great waters. He bore the title "Lord of the Watery Deep." According to some traditions, he—not Marduk—was the creator of all things and more important than Marduk himself. Enki was considered to be both wise and kindly disposed toward mankind, whom he taught both the art of writing and geometry. He it is who was supposed to have warned the Babylonian Noah to build an ark as a place of safety against the impending flood, and his cult had settled here in Eridu in ancient times.

Because of the extensive use of sun-dried brick, buildings in this land—unless well protected by outer walls of baked and glazed brick or tile—were not permanent and, unless kept in constant repair, had to be entirely reconstructed every forty years or so; and it was this full reconstruction that occupied the attention of Nebuchadnezzar's best architects and engineers at the present time.

It was not difficult to spot Nebo-tsabit. Suntanned and bare to the waist, he was on a high scaffold in violent argument with some of his assistants. Holding a sheet of Egyptian papyrus in his left hand, he would first point to the drawings inscribed on it and then turn and scratch into the mud brick wall beside him a new plan or some illustration of a detail not shown on the papyrus. Finally one of his assistants, eager to put an end to this lecture, with considerable diffidence called his attention to the group of visitors standing on the muddy ground below. Nebo-tsabit inclined his head in acknowledgment of our presence, waved the partially rolled up plans in greeting, and with a final word of instruction began to descend the scaffold with great agility. I had known him slightly for several years and found him a man to my liking. He inquired after the king's health and then asked the purpose of our visit, taking it for granted that we came as Nebuchadnezzar's messengers. I suggested that perhaps we could retire to some shady place where the ground was dry and where writing and drawing materials were available. He led us into the portion of the temple already roofed and nearly complete where a room had been set up as a construction office for him with a stool and chairs and tables. My guards took a position at the door as if they were expecting an attack by foreign invaders, and the others—with the exception of Belzephon—remained outside.

As concisely as possible I tried to explain to this gifted man something of what it was that the king had in mind. His immediate reaction was that I was joking, but as it became clear to him that Nebuchadnezzar was entirely serious about this matter, he came to listen more and more intently. By now I had been around Nebuchadnezzar's court long enough to acquire a little sense of what makes a man a good courier and was, therefore, very careful not to let it be known that the suggestion for the building of a garden in the sky was originally my idea, being quite sure that the king would soon come to the conviction that the whole concept had originated with him.

He began to make sketches in a large tray of softened clay which covered the top of a table, now and then stopping to rub out a line with a damp finger and substitute another. After an hour or so we both had to admit that nothing was coming of the effort.

"There are so many problems," Nebo-tsabit pointed out. "There must be great strength to carry the weight of earth deep enough to take the roots of full-grown trees, and we will have to devise a system of bringing water to the topmost story; but," he smiled, "if Nebuchadnezzar wants it, we have to give it to him, don't we? So there must be a way to do it."

It took him two days to get the work on Enki's temple organized so it could progress well in his absence. He delegated authority to the most trustworthy of his assistants whose chief task, now that the plans were drawn and the work was under construction, would be simply to see that the plans were followed and that all went as designed.

On the morning of the third day, we began the return trip up river to Babylon with Nebo-tsabit and two men generally considered the best engineers in the kingdom accompanying us. The trip passed quickly as we discussed the design of what we came to call "the man-made mountain" while the engineers were calculating problems in mass and weight or working to devise a means of lifting water to the summit. Surprisingly, by the time we tied up at the palace wharf, the general concept was pretty well worked out.

The final building was to consist of five or six levels, each tall enough to bring the topmost level well above the height of the city walls to which the building was to be adjacent. Unlike a ziggurat, however, these levels were set off-center of the main base and foundation, providing setbacks on three sides but an almost vertical rise from the first level to the topmost level on the north side in the direction of the city walls. Since brick—even if thoroughly baked—could not carry the weight of the upper stories, it was necessary to import stone slabs from the mountainous region of the north, floating them down on rafts. These were all cut to the proper size according to the exact specifications of the architects, each carefully numbered to conform to the place for which it was designed. The front of the terraces—that is, the south sides— were supported on stone columns and open in that direction, thus providing a series of covered porches which could be filled with flowers and shrubs. The open portions of the terraces were covered to twice a man's height with rich loam and fertile earth, also brought down the rivers. This earth was laid over a floor of lead, which rested on a deep layer of bitumen, which in turn was poured upon straw laid over supporting stone slabs.

Behind the porches on most of the levels were rooms to which the queen and her ladies could withdraw for a nap in the heat of the afternoon or, indeed, even spend the night. On other levels, the space was taken over for cages of wild beasts of various sorts while tame deer were allowed to wander at will in the shade of the tall trees planted all the way to the topmost level. Steps were provided on the east and west ends of the covered areas. Underneath the entire structure were stone foundations with narrow, open corridors and duct work in them through which water flowed, brought up from the river by a series of buckets on a continuous belt which, through an ingenious system of gears, could be turned by mules walking in a circle. A similar system took the water from the basement all the way to the very top, though it was possible to adjust the buckets so that they could be emptied at any level as water was needed. The operation of this system required the service of numerous slaves and a number of beasts. In addition, some fifty or more gardeners were required to fertilize, trim, and generally care for the growing plants.

Not only were ornamental birds kept in large cages under the porches of the towering building, but soon wild birds, attracted by the tall trees in a land where such giants of the forest were unknown, began to build their nests in the branches.

Under Nebuchadnezzar's direction, it required some eight years to realize fully the finished plan. By that time Amytis had so greatly improved in her spirits that she really no longer needed this artificial mountain garden to remind her of Media and the days of her girlhood there. I think it was more to please her husband than for any other reason that she went here almost every afternoon to take a rest and to spend some hours walking in the shade of the trees and admiring the flowers.

The fame of this edifice, commonly called "The Hanging Gardens of Babylon," spread throughout the world. I considered the name unfortunate since men came from faraway places expecting to see a garden hung by chains from the sky; but this structure increased the prestige of great Babylon to the ends of the earth, and the king came to take great delight in showing his important foreign visitors the wonders of the structure. Although I never heard of its happening, I do not doubt that there must have been some elderly ambassadors who suffered heart attacks from climbing all the stairs.

Meantime, Abednego had won the heart and hand of Leah, and they were married in the garden of my house. Nebuchadnezzar, in profound good humor, honored us with his presence, bringing Queen Amytis with him. The queen gave the bride a necklace of carnelian and lapis lazuli, and the king presented Abednego with a magnificent two-year-old stallion. Old friends from Judah, living now in captivity, as well as Babylonian officials who felt it worthwhile to cultivate our favor, were present. As far as I could tell, Leah seemed well-tamed and tractable and appeared to make him a good wife. The old fire was there but well contained; and when a year and a half later she bore Abednego twin sons, she proved herself a most gentle and devoted mother.

The romance between Rachel and Belzephon had not followed an easy course. Belzephon had asked me if I would go with him to her father to stand as sponsor when he asked her father for her hand in marriage. The old priest gave his consent willingly enough, but before the marriage knot could be tied, a serious obstacle presented itself.

Unfortunately, it was one for which I felt some responsibility.

Queen Amytis had sent for me several times, and I had gone to the palace to answer her questions about my God. She inquired earnestly about every aspect of our faith—the meaning of the sacrifices, the office of the priesthood, the laws that God had given. She wanted to talk about Abraham and the patriarchs. I found that this interest stemmed from the fact that as a young girl she had had a Hebrew nurse, a descendant of those Israelites who had been taken captive to Assyria almost 200 years before. These Israelite people had been scattered through the Assyrian empire, and very few, if any, had managed through the generations since to maintain their Jewish traditions. But Amytis's childhood nurse had been full of fragments of information about the religion of her forefathers now, more often than not, mixed with legends and misinformation that had accrued to them over the years. Nebuchadnezzar's queen had never forgotten these stories nor lost interest in them, and she was determined that she would untangle the truth from legend. She had an historian's interest in the records of the past and the desire, I believe God-given, to discover truth.

On the occasion of one of my visits to her, she asked if I could procure from among the captives a refined and well-taught Jewish girl who could spend a few weeks with her as an attendant so she could observe Jewish womanhood at close range and have someone at hand who could answer questions as they occurred to her. I assured the queen that I would procure such a Jewish maiden and, of course, thought immediately of Rachel. I obtained her father's consent and hers; and it was while she was living in the palace that she unfortunately came to the attention of Nabonidus, who was married to Nitocris, a daughter of Nebuchadnezzar, born to an Egyptian princess of the same name.

Nabonidus was captivated by the beauty and modest charm of Rachel and determined to add her to his harem. Though he had only seen her once at a royal banquet where she was in attendance upon Queen Amytis, he was determined to have her. He sought the consent of Amytis to take this lovely woman as a concubine or even as a wife. Amytis in turn discussed this proposal with Rachel, knowing in advance what her reaction would be. In tears, Rachel begged Amytis to refuse Nabonidus's suit and poured out to the kind-hearted queen her love for Belzephon. As long as she remained in the queen's apartments Rachel was beyond the reach of Nabonidus. As is true of all courts, spies abounded in the king's palace; and some of those in the pay of Nabonidus had orders to notify him immediately if Rachel sought to leave the palace.

In fairness I should note that this infatuation was not characteristic of the king's son-in-law. Though a general in the army and active in administrative affairs, Nabonidus was not by nature a lustful or licentious man; and, indeed, he was more interested in discovering the secrets of the past than he was in the events of the present. Everywhere he went he sought to dig up relics of ancient civilizations and fragments of columns, of pottery, and of statuary. He had inherited this scholarly interest from his mother, who was the high priestess of the temple of the moon god Sin in Harran, where she had erected a building in which such objects could be displayed; and antiquarians came from miles around to view them. When he set his sights on an ancient object, he sought to obtain it at any cost, and woe be to any man who sought to thwart him in his desire.

Now for the first time, as far as it was known, he manifested the same obsession to acquire a living object of beauty and youth. All we could do was to urge Belzephon to exercise patience and not give way to some foolish action that could cost him his life and assure him that God would in due time provide a solution to his problem.

In Judah old follies were being reenacted. Zedekiah had made alliances with the new Pharaoh, and formed a confederacy with other neighboring countries to throw off the yoke of Babylon. With more patience than we had attributed to him, Nebuchadnezzar ordered Zedekiah to come to Babylon to answer for this defection.

Prior to Zedekiah's arrival, Nebuchadnezzar said to me, "Another relative of yours is coming to Babylon shortly."

I replied, "I hope he will be welcome."

"That depends on how he promises to behave," replied the king. He then spoke of his concern over the reports he had received about Zedekiah's disloyalty to Babylon.

"Would it please the king for me to warn him against such a course? I know him very slightly—and only when I was a child—but will do what I can to reason with him, if it is your pleasure for me to do so."

It pleased Nebuchadnezzar, and I spent some time with Zedekiah. I found him a very slippery character, and what God showed me of his heart was not matched by his speech, but Zedekiah managed somehow to satisfy Nebuchadnezzar of his loyalty and was allowed to return to Jerusalem.

With the coming of Pharaoh Hophra to the throne of Egypt, open rebellion broke out, and the prophet Ezekiel described Zedekiah's declension in these words: "He rebelled against him by sending ambassadors to Egypt that they might give him horses and a large army." Nebuchadnezzar, now thoroughly aroused, set out again with his army toward the west; and soon the whole countryside, except the cities of Azekah, Lachish, and Jerusalem, were under Babylonian control. Egypt made a feeble attempt to come to the aid of her ally, and for a while the Babylonian armies which were besieging Jerusalem were forced to withdraw their forces in order to meet the Egyptian advance. The Egyptian force retreated to the land of the Nile, and the siege of Jerusalem was resumed. Famine and pestilence ravaged the city before the walls were finally breached and Nebuchadnezzar's army poured into Jerusalem. King Zedekiah attempted to flee, hoping to find a place of sanctuary in Ammon; however, he was captured near Jericho and brought before Nebuchadnezzar, who was engaged in a campaign in Riblah in central Syria. His sons were executed before his eyes; then Zedekiah was blinded and brought back to Babylon in chains.

Finally, the city of Jerusalem was leveled and the remaining treasures of the Temple and all those of the palaces were carted away by the conquerors. Thus ended the kingdom of Judah.

A temporary capital was set up at Mizpah. It was, in fact, a military government under Gedaliah, a Judean appointed by Nebuchadnezzar to represent Babylonian authority. Before departing, the Babylonian general commanded Gedaliah to provide for the safety of Jeremiah, for whom they had tremendous respect since he had warned the Jews what would happen if they dared defy Babylon.

The Jews in Babylon heard the reports of the destruction of Jerusalem and the final overthrow of their kingdom with great sorrows and loud lamentings. Many of them had expected the captivity to be of short duration and were unwilling to put down their roots and establish their lives in this strange country to which God's judgment had brought them. Now, however, with

Jerusalem in ruins and a military government in their homeland, they listened more readily to Ezekiel who warned them that the captivity would last for seventy years. Some began to buy land or go into business while still retaining their identity as Jews and continuing to live, for the most part, in close proximity to their fellow exiles. Except for the very oldest among them, they began to learn Aramaic, the language of the people among whom they lived, something that heretofore many had considered unnecessary in view of their hopes of a short exile. Coming to the realization that only the youngest among them would live to return with their children to Zion, they still clung to their hope that one day their Temple would be rebuilt.

I was not in Babylon when the army returned with its captives and its treasures. Nebuchadnezzar had sent dispatches ordering me to make a tour of inspection of the northernmost provinces, spending some time in each of the major cities in consultation with the satraps and the heads of the military garrisons. I was also to note the conditions of the temples and the attitudes of the various priests, bringing back a full report on all that I discovered and my recommendations as to what needed to be done to improve conditions in each place. I was instructed to take with me my household guards under the direction of Belzephon and such servants and scribes as I would need. My house in Babylon was to be closed, and the king assured me that my property would be protected by the city authorities in my absence. I understood that Nebuchadnezzar wanted me out of Babylon when he returned with his booty and his captives from Jerusalem, having left my boyhood home in ruins, my Temple destroyed, and my kingdom no more than a military outpost of Babylon. I found it difficult to attribute this to any delicacy of feeling on his part; and, puzzled over the reason for it, I thought how little Nebuchadnezzar had come to know me in these years I had served him here. Although my heart was heavy for the destruction of Jerusalem, the crops destroyed, the thousands dead, and the end of the kingdom and the house of my God, I knew these were judgments from God upon a sinful nation that had forgotten the author of its glories and the protector of its shrine; and I could feel no more bitterness toward the king who had been the instrument of that judgment than I could blame the inanimate weapon, a sword or an arrow, that struck down a friend in battle.

In any case, I had finished my trip as the "eye of the king" throughout his realm and returned to Babylon months before Nebuchadnezzar arrived, having sent on ahead the captives and treasures of his conquest. The king had gone directly to besiege Tyre, where he spent two years in attempting to conquer that wealthy port city built half on the shores and half on an island some distance out in the sea itself.

Since Nabonidus was in the west with Nebuchadnezzar, I took advantage of his absence to rescue Rachel permanently from him. Early on the day that we left the city, I stopped at the palace under the pretense of leaving dispatches to be forwarded to the king. While I was visiting my old friend, the chief steward, Rachel joined the group that was to accompany me and quickly mounted one of our extra horses. With Belzephon close beside her on one side, and this royal emissary on the other, we went out northward through the Ishtar Gate. If Nabonidus's spies were still on duty, we either escaped their scrutiny or left them frustrated and unable to interfere.

We followed the course of the Euphrates northward until we came to Sippar at the westward end of the Median Wall, which joined that city on the banks of the Euphrates to Akshak on the Tigris. Nebuchadnezzar had put up this lengthy fortification to protect the city of Babylon from any invasion from the north. Here I had the marriage of Rachel to Belzephon officially registered before the magistrate of the city, and a copy of the records, of course, went to the archives of the city; but a clay tablet with a duplicate record properly sealed went into Belzephon's pouch. In a quiet ceremony in my room in the palace there, I asked God's blessing upon the union and heard them pledge eternal love and faith to each other.

After some days we left Sippar by the road that paralleled the Median Wall to visit Akshak. After accomplishing the inspection here, we moved north to Agade, which lay a short distance to the east of the Tigris. Thence our journey took us to Diyala, Tikrit, Ashur, Nimrud, and finally to Nineveh where I found much of the city unoccupied and overgrown with vegetation. To see this great city, which once ruled so much of the earth, now largely a heap of ruins impressed upon me the futility of all of man's efforts and the limitations put upon his achievements by the judgments of

God and the passing of the years.

By now we had been gone from Babylon well over a year, and the baskets of clay tablets had grown very heavy, and the papyrus scrolls were more than one man could carry. Turning southward again, we reached Kar-tukulti-Ninurta, where we embarked on boats and barges for the trip down the Tigris as far as Lagash. After our sojourn there, we went a short distance westward to Umma and from thence to Ur and finally to Erech and Larsa on the Euphrates. Thence we continued north by that river, returning to Babylon almost two years after we had departed.

This inspection trip as the "eye of the king" had given me a splendid opportunity to collect ancient artifacts, inscriptions, pottery, and statues. These I had discovered by digging exploratory trenches in the ruins of temples and fortifications in the open country and by purchases from collectors here and there. In fact, one whole wagonload of such objects which I had sent months ago from the north awaited my arrival in Babylon, and we brought with us two pack animals loaded with other objects picked up on the return journey.

When Nabonidus returned some months later with Nebuchadnezzar's army, I made him a present of these objects together with so many compliments for his scholarship and wide knowledge as an antiquarian that he quite forgot any slight his self-importance might have suffered at the loss of Rachel, if, indeed, he had not completely forgotten her by then. At least, there were enough inscriptions to occupy his interest for some time to come, together with the difficulty of properly dating and identifying the rest of the artifacts, one of which he insisted antedated the great flood. He was, at best, an eccentric man, and my own personal feeling was that he was quite mad.

In my position, all sorts of rumors came my way. But unlike men in a similar position, I did not employ paid spies and informers, trusting rather in the God of heaven to make known to me the things I needed to know and to expose to my gaze the secrets of men's hearts.

I had sensed on my recent journey that something strange was afoot on the plain between the two rivers. I could think of no special significance of this area—a strange, wild place—where dark oil bubbled out of the ground and eternal flames burned where there were no visible fuels to fire them. We had passed through the area, as I was eager to see this strange phenomenon as well as the bitumen lakes from which came the tarry and waterproof substance used as mortar in the laying of bricks in Babylon and the other cities of the kingdom. As we passed through this desolate landscape, we were conscious of a strange, unpleasant smell so strong in some spots that it almost choked us.

Immediately upon his return to Babylon, Nebuchadnezzar dispatched some of his weary soldiers, together with leatherworkers, tentmakers, goldsmiths, and artisans of various sorts, to the area.

I had, of course, greeted the king at the Ishtar Gate upon his return to the city, paid my duty call to him in the palace, and was one of the honored guests—along with Meshach, Shadrach, and Abednego—at a banquet for the governors of the city.

All of the written reports of my trip of inspection had been deposited in the palace archives; and the king assured me that as he finished reading them or hearing them summarized, he would send for me to hear my suggestions and recommendations for the improvements of conditions throughout the realm. So far I had heard nothing further from him, and there had been no other summons to the palace.

Meantime I learned that Nebuchadnezzar had sent commands throughout the empire to all of the important governmental and military authorities to come to the dedication of an image which the king had erected.

The Babylonian group was by far the largest of all the delegations summoned to the Plain of Dura from throughout the empire. When they arrived, they found a city of tents awaiting them. Servants under the supervision of eunuchs indicated to each where he was to lodge, and a banner bearing his name was placed on a pole in front of the tent. In the center of this circling camp was the royal pavilion, and nearby were tents for cooking and a pavilion large enough to shade the tables where meals for these several thousand officials were to be served.

On the plain outside the camp, there was room for all of those assembled to be seated in comfort on carpets facing the huge image sixty cubits high, which on the king's orders had been erected on a base some six cubits in height so that everyone could have a clear and unhampered view of this remarkable object. The rumor was that it was solid gold; and, indeed, it appeared to be, though I doubt if all the treasures Nebuchadnezzar had brought back to the city in his entire reign would have provided enough of the precious yellow metal to cast a solid statue of that size. I learned later from some of the craftsmen who had helped to construct the image that only the head and hands were of solid gold; the rest of the image had been cast in thin sections and mounted upon an iron frame covered with cedar wood.

The evening banquet, served long before sunset, was accompanied by entertainers of various sorts, including an orchestra, singers, and dancers. It was full dark when a herald announced that all those at the tables should move out to find seats on the carpets facing the image.

If it had looked magnificent and impressive glittering in the light of the afternoon sun or highlighted with the tints of the sunset reflected in the gold, by night it was awesome. Between the statue and the place where the officers and nobles of the kingdom were seated was a wide space where a number of the flames burned up from fissures in the earth, fueled by underground gases. Each of these had been shielded from the eyes of the spectators by a silver reflector which threw the image into high relief. The gigantic figure seemed to move and breathe in the flickering light of these almost supernatural flares. There was something both frightening and awe-inspiring in the sight of this tremendous image of Nebuchadnezzar, for it had been, indeed, created by clever workmen into what seemed now a living and breathing likeness of the great king.

No one dared speak aloud, and so intent was the silence that you could hear the roaring of lions in the distance and the cries of night birds attracted by the light. Then a trumpet sounded, and the voice of the herald sounded, amplified by a speaking trumpet that carried his words to the very back row and could be plainly heard by the servants, the guards, the slaves, and the workers and tentmakers who were responsible for this remarkable and impermanent city and who now stood behind the seated officials.

"To you it is commanded, all people, nations, and languages, that when you hear the sound of the cornet, flute, harp, sackbut, psaltery, dulcimer, and other instruments of music that you shall fall down and worship the golden image that Nebuchadnezzar the king has set up. And whosoever does not fall down and worship shall at once be cast into the midst of the burning fiery furnace."

Having spoken first in Aramaic, the herald now repeated the same announcement in all of the various languages and dialects of the widespread kingdom of Nebuchadnezzar.

The three Hebrew captives, clothed in their official garments as assistant governors of the province of Babylon, each with his gold chain of office about his neck, had with wise forethought found seats at the very back of the assembled nobles. As the herald was repeating his announcement in the dialects and languages of the realms, the three princes of Judah exchanged glances. Shadrach, who was seated in the center, gave an almost imperceptible nod but one that was plainly understood by his companions.

Now, with the trumpet blast and sound of sweet chords from the harp, the orchestra began to play a moving melody that combined the stirring excitement of an urgent call to battle with the seductive cadence of a hymn to a Babylonian god. Some two thousand men of highest rank and importance fell face down in obeisance to the image while behind them not a steward, a eunuch, or a servant remained standing.

Only Meshach, Shadrach, and Abednego had

remained quietly seated upon their carpets, their hands reposing quietly upon their thighs. Had they been lesser men, they might have reasoned in themselves and found some excuse or justification for disobeying the second commandment. They were not being asked to turn from the worship of God but only to bow to this image. The king who commanded this act was their lawful sovereign, and they were pledged to obey his commandments; therefore, the sin would be his, not theirs. Or they might have reasoned that Nebuchadnezzar had been almost like a father to them, giving them honors and positions of importance, and gratitude demanded that they follow his wishes. Or yet again the argument might have been that they could save their lives and retain their high position in which they were able to render some benefits to the Jewish captives living in the province of Babylon. These excuses were no inducement to disregard the commandment of their God who had declared, "Thou shalt not make unto thee any graven image, or any likeness of any thing that is in heaven above, or that is in the earth beneath, or that is in the water under the earth. Thou shalt not bow down thyself to them, nor serve them."

Their unwillingness to disobey the command of God and bow in reverence before an image made by hands had not gone unnoticed. Though neither the king himself on his raised throne nor most of the assembled crowd had observed it, this had not escaped the eye of Nergal-Zakiru, the chief magician who, bending almost double to avoid attracting attention, worked his way to a place where a group of Chaldeans was seated and dropping down among them began to whisper. The Chaldeans turned to cast hate-filled glances toward the three Hebrews. After a hurried consultation the three Chaldeans of highest rank stood to their feet and, adjusting their garments carefully, approached the throne of the king where they abased themselves in the most fawning of obeisances.

Never prone to brevity, the dean began by reminding the king of his decree and of his sentence upon all those who failed to bow down, and concluded with the words, "There are certain Jews whom you have set over the affairs of the province of Babylon—Shadrach, Meshach, and Abednego—but these men, O King, have not regarded you. They do not serve your gods nor worship the golden image which you have set up."

His two companions now joined in, expressing their indignation that the king's person should be so lightly regarded and that men in high place should show so little gratitude to the man to whom they owed their position.

Gripped by one of his sudden fits of intense rage, Nebuchadnezzar commanded that Shadrach, Meshach, and Abednego be brought before him. By the time they had been dragged to the dais and flung down before his feet, the king had regained something of his composure. These three were men who had served faithfully and never failed to demonstrate their loyalty and regard for him.

"Do you not serve my gods or worship the golden image which I have set up?" he inquired.

Before they could reply, he continued. "Perhaps you did not understand the decree, but I shall give you another opportunity. If you are ready now, when you hear the sound of the cornet, flute, harp, sackbut, psaltery, dulcimer, and all of the instruments of the orchestra, to fall down and worship the image which I have made, it shall be well for you. But if you do not worship it, you shall be cast immediately into the midst of the burning fiery furnace; and who is that God that shall deliver you out of my hands?"

Shadrach was the first to answer, speaking quietly and respectfully. "Nebuchadnezzar, we are not afraid to answer you frankly about this. If it be His will, our God whom we serve is able to deliver us from a burning fiery furnace, and He will deliver us out of your hand, O King."

Now the tall young man Abednego declared in his deep voice loud enough to be heard by all of the assembly, "But if not, then know, O King, that we will not serve your gods or worship the golden image which you have set up."

Now Nebuchadnezzar lost all control. Rising to his feet, his face red with anger, he shouted in a rage that the furnace should be heated seven times hotter than it was generally kept. He called to the burly guards standing nearby, ordering them to bind Shadrach, Meshach, and Abednego and cast them into the burning heat of the furnace.

A short distance away there was a remarkable

phenomenon. A great ring of blue fire sprang up out of the ground, the circle complete except for an opening perhaps one eighth of its circumference. This strange phenomenon was known far and wide as the fiery furnace. This flame out of the earth was believed by the superstitious to be the flames of hell breaking through the crust of the earth.

Years ago, in an effort to see if the fires could be extinguished, a band of wandering desert dwellers had attempted to smother it with sand. Instead of extinguishing the fire, the sand caused the circle to grow smaller; but no amount of effort could extinguish it entirely. A limit in the circumference was finally reached where any sand thrown upon the flames would be lifted by the force of the gases and thrown back hot into the face of those pouring on the sand. This remarkable characteristic of the fiery circle had become widely known in the years since it was first discovered, and there were tales of curious creatures, half man and half beast, that came here at the time of the new moon to offer sacrifices to some strange and hideous god, casting the bound victim into the center of the circle, and then moving the fire close to him by pouring on sand. Even when the circle was at its greatest extent, the heat within was of great intensity and, when it was forced down to its smallest circumference, was immeasurably hot.

Now soldiers were busy shoveling earth upon the circle from without, forcing it to become smaller and smaller. Just as the mighty men approached to throw Shadrach, Meshach, and Abednego into the fire, this effort to limit its size suddenly caused it to blaze up to twice its usual height, and it seemed to reach out fiery arms to embrace those who were casting in God's servants. As they tried to draw back, in the sight of all the watching eyes, they burst into flame and fell like burning logs to the ground, their helmets and their armor warped and melted by the heat; but inside the fiery walls Meshach, Shadrach, and Abednego were untouched. The only thing burned away was the cords with which they had been bound. They walked and talked together, their hats still on their heads.

Astonished and confused, Nebuchadnezzar cried out to those beside him, "Did we not cast three bound men into the middle of the fire?"

"We did, O King," they answered.

But Nebuchadnezzar in a frenzy cried, "Look, I see four men loose, walking there in the midst of the fire, unhurt; but the form of the fourth is like the Son of God!"

Clear to the eyes of all was the shining rainbow brilliance of that fourth figure. Then Nebuchadnezzar, drawing as near as he dared to the narrow opening in the flaming circle, cried, "Shadrach, Meshach, and Abednego, servants of the Most High God, come forth! Come!"

The three Hebrews, as obedient servants of the king, walked out of the midst of the fire to the astonishment of the princes, the governors, the captains, and the king's counselors who were gathered there. The fire had had no power upon them. Not a hair of their heads was singed, and there was no smell of the fire upon them.

Then Nebuchadnezzar blessed the God of Shadrach, Meshach, and Abednego for sending an angel and delivering His servants that trusted in Him, men who dared to defy the king's word rather than serve or worship any god except their own. Calling for the herald, he declared, "I make a decree that every people, nation, and language which blasphemes against the God of Shadrach, Meshach, and Abednego shall be cut in pieces; and their houses shall be made a dunghill because there is no other god who can deliver like this."

The king promoted Shadrach, Meshach, and Abednego to places of even greater power and honor in the province of Babylon. So God mocked the pride of the king who shortly after had the golden image melted down and brought back in ingots to the treasury of Babylon.

Few men in the city of tents slept well that night, and early in the morning they began to disperse each to his own city, province, and kingdom. The word of the power of the God of heaven was scattered abroad everywhere along with the king's decree forbidding any man upon pain of death to speak amiss about the God of Shadrach, Meshach, and Abednego.

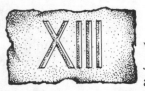

When I heard from my Jewish brothers the account of the miracle that God had performed, I felt a variety of emotions. The first of these was a sense of regret that I had not been present to share with them this opportunity to witness to the faithfulness of the Lord and to look upon the angel likeness of the Son of God in the midst of the fire. Then I knew a great upsurge of pity for Nebuchadnezzar whose pride had led him to this foolish and extravagant display which had ended so disastrously for him.

I think I understood something of his motives. The boundaries of his empire were now spread so far and embraced so many subject kingdoms whose conquered people could not but hate their conqueror that he had sought to devise something which could command a common loyalty. It must impress upon them the magnificence and power of the empire of which they were, though even reluctantly, a part. He was too wise to think he could replace the gods of these conquered nations with the deities of Babylon and bring them under the loyalty of a common religion. To have attempted such a thing would have ringed Babylon in with fires of revolution everywhere, for in nothing are men so intolerant as in matters of religion; on the other hand, he reasoned, if he could present himself, the king, as a living god, a god-man, a sort of common deity which all could embrace without abandoning their native deities, that might accomplish the purpose of strengthening the empire.

From the reports that were constantly coming to me from distant lands and from what I had observed on my trip of investigation, this seeming solid and magnificent edifice of government had cracks in its foundations like those that appear in the brick foundations of an impressive building following a flood. I prayed that the episode on the Plain of Dura would cause the king to turn from pride to the God of heaven, but in the days and weeks that followed, I saw no sign of any change. He had decreed that no man might blaspheme this God who did such great wonders but was not willing to trust Him personally.

Meshach, Shadrach, and Abednego had been promoted to higher honors and greater responsibilities. I remained in my position as the chief counselor of the king with the title of the governor of the province of Babylon and the ruler of all the wise men, soothsayers, and magicians of the city; but I was rarely called on for advice when decisions were made.

I was particularly concerned, however, about the rapid promotion of a man named Gubaru to high office in the army. Belzephon, who was about his age and knew him well, considered him treacherous and unreliable. On the few occasions when I met him, I found him a man of great charm and force of personality; but I had a most strange experience the first time he came to pay a visit in his full military garb. It seemed that the breastplate he wore and the helmet he had placed on the floor beside his chair faded and changed; and he seemed clothed in the silver-chased armor of a Persian general with the helmet of a Persian commander by his side and appeared to age to a man in his sixties. All this was but a matter of a moment, but I knew that Belzephon was right. Here was a man who in years to come would betray Babylon to its enemies, but I was given assurance that in those years our lives would be somehow intertwined.

It was only much later that I learned that Gubaru was the youngest son of Cyaxares, the king of the Medes, who had joined forces with Nebuchadnezzar in the conquest of Nineveh; and I could readily understand why he was so highly favored by the Babylonian king.

As the years passed, each seemingly more swiftly than the one that had gone before, I tried to discharge faithfully the responsibilities placed upon me. Meantime, King Zedekiah died in prison having never recovered from the ordeal of seeing his sons slain before he was blinded. No announcement was made of his death, and I learned of it from the eunuch who was entrusted to see that his body was cremated and the ashes scattered outside the city walls.

Several times I had sent petitions to the king asking for permission to remove my aunt and cousin from their house near Tel-Abib to more spacious quarters in the city or elsewhere. The first two petitions, sent some six months apart, were ignored; and I was informed in answer to the third some months later, "Nebuchadnezzar has determined that the captive king Jehoiachin and his mother shall remain where they are, nor can they leave the house where they are living on the king's bounty."

During these years Nebuchadnezzar was several times out of Babylon, busy somewhere with a military campaign. As important as they were, these expeditions were regarded by the king as unfortunate interruptions to his building and engineering projects—not the least of which was the altering of the course of the Euphrates as it approached Babylon from the north, so that instead of following its direct course, it was forced to take a serpentine route which required a boat approaching the city to pass in sight of the walls some five times before reaching the city itself, the purpose being to provide a series of water barriers which must be crossed by an invading army.

Meantime, Tyre had fallen after a siege of thirteen years, and Nebuchadnezzar had fought against Pharaoh Amasis on the borders of Egypt with no decisive results on either side.

The two things that touched me most directly were not recorded in the annals of the kingdom. In the thirty-fifth year of the king's reign—which was, of course, according to Hebrew reckoning, our thirty-sixth year as captives—the prophet Ezekiel died and was buried in the cemetery which the Jewish captives had established for themselves a Sabbath day's journey southeast of Tel-Abib.

Almost exactly two years later we buried Abednego nearby, but on the stone above his grave was carved in Hebrew characters the name Azariah. He had been taken with a sudden illness and high fever, and the messenger brought word to us as we sat at supper one evening. I sent servants to summon Shadrach and Meshach to meet me at Abednego's house where we sat beside him all night, bathing him with cool cloths, for the heat was intense. Having no faith in Chaldean physicians, we ministered to him ourselves doing everything possible.

Shortly before sunrise the fever left him, and he awoke from the coma. Leah, now a striking woman in the prime of life, her hair touched with gray, was supporting his head against her breast, and their twin sons were one on either side of their father. Meshach, Shadrach, and I stood near his feet. Belzephon and Rachel were side by side against the wall near the door, Rachel weeping silently. Azariah smiled at us in turn and extended a hand to be clasped by each of his tall sons—one so much like him and the other so much like their mother. He was gone just as the first rays of the sun began to climb the eastern horizon.

According to the custom of our country, we washed and anointed his body before wrapping it in strips of cotton cloth. We took the body with us on a vessel down the river as far as we could, carrying it on a bier from there to the cemetery. His closest associates, his servants, and his secretaries had followed the funeral barge down the river in other vessels and now went with us in the procession to the burial place.

As we finished digging the grave, the sun moved into eclipse; and we buried him in darkness. The eclipse passed, and the sun shone brightly above the western horizon as we finished filling the grave. It was thirty-eight years since he had left Jerusalem.

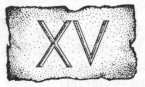XV Although Nebuchadnezzar was no longer a young man, he was still possessed of such vitality and ambition that it seemed only the God of heaven could limit his conquests. By now almost all of the dreams of his youth were realized. He had added to his kingdom Arabia, parts of Egypt, Judea, Syria, and Phoenicia after the fall of Tyre. He had not yet realized his dream for opening trade routes to India, but he was still determined that all of the riches of India should be funneled through his capital city on their way to the north and west. He believed India men could pick up precious and semi-precious stones, harvesting them like barley growing on the banks of the Euphrates. Also, India was a land of spices including cinnamon, that strange bark which was believed to be taken by birds to their nests and stolen from them by men. But there was little trade with India, something the king was determined to change.

Heretofore most of the merchandise from Arabia had been bound via the Red Sea and Sinai for the country of the Phoenicians, from which the precious goods could be taken by ship across the Great Sea and even through the narrow gates to the western ocean and sold to the dwellers on the misty isles. He was determined that the traffic to cities like Aden and Yemen should be rerouted to the northern end of the Persian Gulf and thence up the river past Babylon. He was busy building new canals to make it possible for the largest of trade ships to find good harbor. He was seeking to make the Euphrates navigable far to the north of Babylon so that caravans carrying the goods brought by water from India could reach the Mediterranean by the shortest route. For several years he had been building a great port at the head of the Persian Gulf which, in its size and the number of its docks, would put other ports to shame. Had he not established so effective an administration in the province of Babylon with its various delegations of power, the king would not have been able to spend so much time away on military expeditions to enlarge his kingdom.

On one of these increasingly rare occasions when he was in Babylon, I was surprised when the king summoned me in haste to the palace, for I had not seen him for months except at a distance. Now, as years ago when I so rashly forced myself into his presence, this summons also concerned the interpretation of a dream, but this time it was a dream well remembered by the great king.

He began by explaining that he had sent for the magicians, the astrologers, the Chaldeans, and the soothsayers and told them the nature of his dream, but none of them could make known unto him the interpretation. In other words, he had sent for me in desperation and as a last resort. He begged me to tell him the meaning of the dream, stating that he knew that the Spirit of the Holy God was in me and that no secret troubled me. Again my heart went out to this great sovereign in pity; and praying silently that God would give me the interpretation of the dream I prepared myself to listen to the king describe it, all the time feeling a strange sense of foreboding and unease as to what this dream might portend.

"I was having a vision as I lay sleeping," he began, "and I saw a great tree in the midst of the earth, so tall that it seemed to reach unto heaven, and its branches stretched to the ends of all the earth as it grew strong. It had beautiful leaves and great fruit in which there was food enough for all flesh. Under the shadow of the tree, the beasts of the field were gathered, and the birds of heaven built their nests in the branches. Man and beast and bird were fed on the fruit of that tree. In my vision a watcher and an holy one came down from heaven. The watcher cried aloud, 'Cut down the tree and cut off his branches. Shake off his leaves and scatter his fruit. Let the beasts get out from under it and the fowls from his branches. But leave the stump of his roots in the earth, even with a band of iron and brass in the young grass of the field, and let it be wet with the dew of heaven. Set his portion with the beasts in the grass of the earth. Let his heart be changed from a man's heart to a beast's heart, and let seven years pass over him.' Finally he said, 'This is by decree of the watchers and the demand by the word of the holy ones, in order that the living may know that the Most High ruleth in the kingdom of men and giveth it to whomever He will and setteth up before it the lowest kind of men.' "

As he finished describing his dream, he appealed to me again to make known unto him the interpretation because, he repeated, "The spirit of the holy gods is in you."

I remained standing before the king, my head bowed and my heart heavy, knowing as the interpretation was revealed to me that my forebodings had been justified. The king sat in silence, evidently believing that my hesitancy to speak was a waiting upon the Lord to reveal the dream.

Then he must have begun to sense that the dream boded evil for him, for he spoke saying, "Belteshazzar, do not let this dream or the interpretation of it distress you."

Slowly I answered, "My lord, this dream will bring rejoicing to them that hate you, and the interpretation of the dream will delight your enemies."

Then I explained what the dream meant. The great tree whose branches spread out over the earth and whose height reached to heaven was Nebuchadnezzar himself. I said, "It is you, O King, who has grown and become strong, and your dominion stretches to the end of the earth. The word of the watcher and the holy one is a judgment of the Most High God, which is passed upon my lord, the king. They shall drive you from men, and you shall live with the beasts of the field. They will make you to eat grass like oxen. They shall wet you with the dews of heaven, and seven years shall pass over you until you recognize that the Most High rules in the kingdom of men and gives it to whomever He will; but since they command to leave the stump of the tree roots, your kingdom will be secured for you after you have known that the heavens rule."

Nebuchadnezzar sat stone-faced, only a slight tick in the corner of his eye marring the impassive countenance. Whether he believed my interpretation and accepted it, I could not tell, but out of my love for this man, I dared to warn him, saying, "O King, accept my advice. Break off your sins by righteousness, and your iniquities by showing mercy to the poor if it may mean a lengthening of your tranquility."

Unresponding, the king stared straight in front of him as I bowed and left the royal presence.

 I lived in a state of constant unease, waiting for the judgment to be hurled at the king. Twelve months I waited, and suddenly it fell. Nebuchadnezzar was showing an ambassador from Egypt the riches of his treasures and the greatness of his capital. Last of all, he took him to the topmost level of the lofty garden edifice. And pointing out from that vantage point the chief features of the city—the extent of its walls, the number of its temples, and the beauty of its palaces—he asked, "Is this not great Babylon that I have built for the kingdom by the might of my power?"

The words were not out of his mouth before the voice of the watcher was heard speaking from heaven: "King Nebuchadnezzar, as it was spoken to you, the kingdom is taken from you. They shall drive you from men, and you shall live with the beasts of the field. They shall make you to eat grass as oxen, and seven years shall pass over you until you know that the Most High rules in the kingdom of men and gives it to whomever He wills."

At once the great king became as a beast,

117

unable to think like a man. In fact, his countenance that had inspired such great reverence and fear in those who looked upon him seemed suddenly to have coarsened. And the dull and stupid eyes and slavering mouth sickened those who looked upon him, and his own courtiers with blows drove him away from them. Finally he wandered out of his palace and eventually out through the gate of the city, dropping behind him the garments he tore off one by one, marking the way he had passed.

That evening, shortly before twilight, a messenger out of breath from running knocked on my door crying, "Queen Amytis summons Belteshazzar to the palace at once."

I found this remarkable woman, even more beautiful in maturity than when I had first met her, seated in the king's chair in the small council chamber. With her were Gubaru and my old friend Arioch, now retired as the captain of the king's guard, his shoulders as straight as ever but his hair like the snows of Lebanon. After I had taken the seat indicated by Amytis, Neriglissar, a counselor of King Nebuchadnezzar and a man who had had a prominent part in the Jerusalem negotiations and was the husband of one of Nebuchadnezzar's many daughters, entered and took his usual place. The last to arrive was Awil-Marduk, a young man and one of the handsomest of Nebuchadnezzar's sons. He was almost as proud of spirit as his father but tender of heart like his mother Queen Amytis.

I was convinced that of all present only Amytis knew the extent of the madness of the king and possessed a complete assurance that he would, at the end of seven years, be restored to his sanity and to his throne. I had come to know that she was one of the lamps of God lighted in Babylon and that she, having heard from Nebuchadnezzar the interpretation of the dream, accepted it as true. Her deep faith gave her great force and strength of character that enabled her to dominate and influence men as diverse as those gathered here. Some were not friendly to others, as I knew from the revelation in my heart that Neriglissar hated Awil-Marduk.

As I pondered on these things, Queen Amytis began to speak in her controlled, well-modulated tones: "All of us here are grieved over the condition of our king, but this has come to pass as was revealed to him in the dream a year ago. According to that same dream as interpreted by Belteshazzar, seven years must pass before he is recovered. I have proclaimed myself regent for the time of the king's illness, and I have brought you here that you may form with me a council for the government of the kingdom. Some of you are related to the king, either by blood or by marriage. The rest of you are trusted friends whom the king has honored with power and position. We must choose someone to act as the head of the armies for the protection and peace of the capital. Others of you shall have special responsibilities as we divide this burden among us."

She then asked if we would stand with her in this time of trouble, and being assured that we would support the kingdom and hold it together, the council agreed to meet the next day after having considered the problems that faced us, hoping that we could at that time formulate a plan of operation.

When Nabonidus returned from Arabia a few months later, he was asked to join the council also. Thanks to Nebuchadnezzar's organizational ability, the machinery of the civil government, though ponderous, would continue to operate efficiently provided the heads of the various departments remained loyal and could be made to realize that graft, corruption, or laziness would not be tolerated but would be dealt with as speedily as they would be were the great king himself in possession of his faculties.

The council asked me to assume the responsibility of checking out the various governors, satraps, mayors, judges, and treasurers throughout the kingdom because I had fairly recently made an inspection tour for Nebuchadnezzar and was known personally to many of them and had earned their respect as a man who, if occasion warranted it, could exercise severe discipline. Shadrach and Meshach were already in positions of authority to do the same within the city and province of Babylon itself. Nabonidus was to take over the military defenses of the city and serve as the commanding general for the province. To Gubaru was entrusted the command of the army to the south. Young Awil-Marduk, though not a seasoned campaigner, had enough experience as his father's lieutenant to be entrusted with the army of the north. Queen Amytis as regent was the final authority in all matters and the one from whose decision there was no appeal.

Some months before God's judgment fell upon her husband, she had confessed to me that she had embraced our faith. I knew that she was in constant touch with the leaders of the Jewish communities and kept the Sabbath in the confines of her own apartment. Although I had every confidence in her wisdom and would have trusted her judgment on almost any matter, she was far too wise a person to act arbitrarily and without the advice of the council unless a sudden emergency should arise and a decision must be made immediately when there was no time to summon the council into session. As long as the crops throughout the kingdom were good and there was no famine or foreign invasion and the army remained loyal, it seemed to me that there were no insurmountable problems ahead. We decided, however, to let it be widely known throughout the kingdom that this illness was a temporary judgment upon the king and that the God of Belteshazzar had promised to restore Nebuchadnezzar to his throne at the end of seven years. This, we felt, would give any who were tempted to rebel a reason to consider matters very carefully before taking action.

We determined that, in a show of confidence, everything should proceed as normally as possible—that the king's building program should go forward providing employment for a great number of Babylonians and that there be no sign of cutting back in any way in the activities that the people of his kingdom had come to expect under the rule of Nebuchadnezzar. Unless we were forced to it, however, there would be no foreign campaigns undertaken, though the army would be kept well-trained and at peak efficiency.

Had Nitocris, Nebuchadnezzar's Egyptian wife, been a woman of different temperament, we might have faced some problems. The daughter of Pharaoh Necho II, she had been a great beauty at the time of her marriage. Now, like many Egyptian women in middle life, she was growing plump, and it was rumored that she was lazy and disinterested in the affairs of the realm. It is true she did not seek to meddle in the government, but she did not have an indolent bone in her well-padded body. Her interests lay in a different direction—in fact, in many directions. She spoke at least five languages and was an authority on the history of necromancy and the black arts, though it should be said in her favor that though extremely curious in these things, she had no wish to become a practitioner of them but rather to expose them as fraudulent. She was also interested in spinning and weaving and had established a school and factory where young women were taught to design and produce textiles widely in demand for their brilliant colors and unusual textures. She was a gifted painter and a better-than-average sculptor who worked in clay. When Nebuchadnezzar wished to particularly honor a visitor from abroad, he would present him with a ceramic portrait-head done from life by Queen Nitocris.

There was no jealousy toward Amytis on the part of the Egyptian consort. In fact, the two queens were more devoted than many sisters. Amytis, being slightly older than Nitocris and already established in Babylon when the Egyptian arrived, took her under her wing, knowing well the pain of adjustment that a foreign princess could face in a land far from her home and among people whose customs and manner of life were different from her own.

The Egyptian's daughter, also named Nitocris and now married to Nabonidus, was unlike her mother but was beyond the shadow of a doubt the daughter of Nebuchadnezzar—like him not only in appearance but in strength and temperament. The only thing she inherited from her mother, apparently, was her artistic bent, but the daughter found her creative outlet in architecture and engineering. Unlike the king, his daughter had abundant time for a thorough study of the art of building; and there was not an engineer in the whole kingdom who could match her when it came to figuring weights and stresses. Those men in the construction trade most prejudiced against the idea of a woman in their field had to acknowledge her ability and soon came to her with technical problems they could not resolve.

The "Babylonian princess," as she was commonly named to distinguish her from her mother the queen, was ambitious, but not to rule the kingdom—only to embellish it and extend its fame by her works in brick and mortar. She readily acceded to Amytis's request that she continue her father's program of construction in Babylon and in some of the other important cities of the kingdom.

She began immediately on what was possibly her crowning achievement—the building of a bridge over the Euphrates near the center of the city, making it possible for the first time to pass all the way across Babylon from east to west without using a boat or swimming. Wisely she designed boat-shaped piers, their pointed ends upstream, so that even during spring floods there would be very little hindrance to the flow of the waters. The bridge was safe and firm under all conditions. However, to prevent the spreading of riots from one section of town to the other— should such a thing ever occur in Babylon—the decking, or walkway, could be removed temporarily.

Neriglissar's presence on the council made it possible for me to become well acquainted with him, and I took advantage of the first opportunity to have a private conversation with this man so recently come from Jerusalem.

That which I had heard from the Jewish captives had caused me great concern for the welfare of the prophet Jeremiah. There seemed to be on the part of most of these men some bitterness toward him because his prophecy of the destruction of the Temple had been fulfilled. To me this seemed as foolish as for a king to put a messenger to death because he brought bad news. I was constantly having to remind my Jewish brethren that it was their sins and their failure to heed the voice of the prophet that brought tragedy to the Holy City and exile to them. In spite of their present situation, many of my countrymen had not learned the lesson that loss of home and exile to a foreign country should have taught them.

I sought to learn from this Neriglissar, one of the conquerors of my people, any facts concerning the state and condition of Jeremiah. What he told me concerning the treatment that the prophet had received at the hands of his countrymen confirmed what I had already heard from some of the captives: he had been mistreated, imprisoned, ridiculed by those to whom God had appointed him to minister. I found, however, that this pagan deeply respected and admired the prophet so unappreciated and hated by his own people.

"He is a most remarkable man," said Neriglissar, "one who does not hesitate to do things that men look upon as foolish when he believes that God commands him to do them."

"When you were in Jerusalem, was he well?" I asked.

"I suppose well enough considering all they had put him through. He looked pale from his imprisonments and thin from fasting," the

Babylonian told me, "but I never knew a man so consumed with zeal and concern for people who abused him and refused to listen to his words. They joke about the fact that he has no religious followers and that all of his years of preaching have not resulted in a single person's being changed."

"But you know, sir, they are wrong about that," I interrupted. "Years ago, a boy about twelve years old heard him preach. He was a young man then, this prophet. His language was both scathing and tender. He reproached his hearers for the pride they took in the Temple while at the same time having so little desire to do the will and obey the commands of the God of the Temple. Jeremiah warned that God would give the land into the hands of conquerors who would destroy the Temple which they themselves had desecrated by their idolatry and sin. The boy who was among his hearers that day made up his mind to serve the God of the Temple and walk in the faith of his fathers."

"You knew this boy?" asked Neriglissar.

"I was that boy," I told him, "and I wish there were some way Jeremiah could know that all of his preaching has not been without fruit."

 Before leaving the city to begin my second trip throughout the kingdom, I made a quiet and unpublicized visit to Tel-Abib, where I had asked certain leading men among the Jews of the exiles to meet me secretly. I explained to these men—most of whom had been prominent in Jerusalem but all of whom were known as faithful and pious Jews, untainted by the corruption of that apostate city in its latter days— the story of Nebuchadnezzar's dream of the great tree and its interpretation, emphasizing the fact that God would at the end of seven years restore Nebuchadnezzar both to his reason and to his throne.

"Some of you," I said, "look upon Nebuchadnezzar as an enemy when you should rather see in him God's instrument of judgment upon us for our sins. Though the Holy City has ceased to exist and the Temple of our God has been leveled, remember His promise that all shall be restored. Here, though exiles, you are treated fairly. Your sons are not slain nor your daughters taken from you. You are permitted, as if you were native-born citizens of Babylon, to establish a life for yourself and to practice the commands of the God of heaven and observe the rites and ceremonies of your Jewish faith. Though God's promise of the king's restoration shall come to pass whether or not you hear my request and grant it, I ask that you assign your sons and grandsons one by one to follow the mad king in his wanderings and protect him from those who might injure or abuse him. Let each in turn give him what shelter he can and keep him in view and, as much as he will permit, serve his needs."

I was pleased to see that for the most part they were responsive to my pleadings, and they established a schedule so that each would take over the surveillance of the king.

Knowing well the nature of my Jewish brethren, I knew there existed among these aliens in a strange country some kind of underground organization and means of communicating quickly to each other such information as was important to the people of the exile. The existence of such a system was confirmed when I asked if anyone knew where the king was at the time. A number of heads nodded, and one young man answered for all: "He was seen today outside the walls of the city toward the southeast; and he seems to be moving generally in this direction, though his wanderings have been so erratic that it is impossible to say where he will be from one day to the next."

Beginning the next day, these children of the

Covenant kept a journal of the wanderings of this unfortunate man until the day that God restored him to his senses. Later when this journal was brought to me, I found it sad reading, and the scrolls were wet with my tears as Nebuchadnezzar had been wet by the dews of heaven during the seven years of his mad wanderings. I was touched by two entries in particular: "Today the king spent most of his time up to his neck in the water of the canal to avoid being bitten by the flies that have so tormented him this season"; but to me the saddest entry of all was this: "The king was grazing today in the garden of Jehoiachin's house when the queen sent a servant to drive him away lest he trample the berry patch or tear down the vines with the young grapes." I hoped from the bottom of my heart that Nebuchadnezzar would have no memory of those seven years during which he lived as the cattle of the field. I was sure that none of us in the council of the kingdom would ever forget them.

Although things moved along almost normally and the well-greased machine operated as smoothly as a good cartwheel turns on a strong axle, there were still some problems—particularly on the distant frontiers of the kingdom where cities were lax in the payment of their tribute and only the threats of the authorities and the presence of our soldiers prevented open rebellion from lifting its head.

In Babylon itself, the greatest problem we faced was with the priests who thought they could take upon themselves new privileges, plucked, as it were, from the grasp of what they felt was the weak government of a woman. Word of Amytis's conversion had been spread through the religious authorities, and she was bitterly hated by the priestesses of Ishtar because of it. Strangely enough, the priests of the goddess did not appear to be as much disturbed as the temple prostitutes, who were undoubtedly shamed by the purity and virtue of Amytis's faith and personal life. It was reported to the authorities of the city that these women were urging men who resorted to them to join a secret conspiracy to murder Amytis, destroy the mad king, and place Nabonidus on the throne. They promised the blessing of Ishtar upon any who joined them in the scheme, one which in any case demanded secrecy rather than an attempt to recruit as many followers as possible, some of whom were sure to reveal the affair.

The queen handled the problem magnificently, sending soldiers to arrest the priestesses and bring them before her in the throne room of the palace. The queen gave them to understand if she heard any further reports that they were trying to disaffect the people or threaten her with the wrath of their goddess, they would have their ears cut off and the royal brand burned into both cheeks. Since no priestess with a blemished countenance could serve Ishtar, it would have been impossible to threaten any punishment more effective. So determined was Queen Amytis to show herself able to hold the realm together and settle its problems satisfactorily that I could not but believe that, as gentle as her nature was, she would not have hesitated to punish rebellion in this fashion, nor would such punishment be considered unduly cruel or extreme in Babylon.

In the fifth year of Nebuchadnezzar's madness, we discovered that the figures on the official army tablets were entirely fictitious. In reality, almost all of the formations were incomplete, and the figures being sent to the council appeared to have been manufactured. In one instance, out of one total assignment of 500 men, we discovered that only 120 remained. The others had died, run away, or gone home. This occurred in the southern army, of which Gubaru was the commander. This situation and others like it had been kept from his attention, or he had ignored the information. It is fortunate that the God of heaven had promised to preserve the kingdom for Nebuchadnezzar, for had we been attacked by a powerful enemy, I do not believe that Babylon would have survived.

I had tried to give the best possible education and training to the twin sons of Abednego and Leah. The firstborn by three minutes, called Sheshbazzar, had a tremendous understanding of mathematics and proved himself a skillful tax assessor in the department of the treasury while his brother Abonizah exhibited strong gifts of leadership and the power to command respect.

I had taken Abonizah with me on one or two of the first trips which I made to check on affairs in other cities in the kingdom; and toward the end of the seven years, I sent him in my place to straighten out problems that had arisen in Harran. He came back with a most interesting report of his confrontation with Shamua-Damqa, the high priestess of the temple of Sin. This formidable woman was the mother of Nabonidus and was especially despised by the priests of Bel Marduk. This enmity, due to a long-time jealousy between the servants of the rival deities, had been inculcated in her son and became an important influence in the fall of Babylon to the Persians some fifteen years later.

Abonizah said, "You have no idea what she is like. Although close to ninety years old, she looks barely sixty, is tall, and her neck is long. Her face, with its aristocratic nose and large eyes, reminded me of some bird of prey; and when she pounced on me, it was with all of the ferocity of an eagle upon a hare. She threatened me not only with the wrath of her deity but with that of Nabonidus also."

"How did you respond?" I inquired.

"I told her politely that as a Jew, I had no fear of her god Sin who did not exist except as a projection of a demon power. I told her that I was the son of one of the men who had walked out of Nebuchadnezzar's fiery furnace and that I enjoyed the protection of Belteshazzar, the governor of the province of Babylon and, moreover, a friend of her son, General Nabonidus. She became quite charming, delivered to me the records you had sent me to procure, and then proceeded to question me as to the source of the power that had protected my father and his friends from the heat of the fiery furnace. I really think she tried to flirt with me at the last."

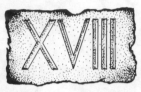

The end of the seventh year of the king's madness was approaching, and so great was the fear of the God of the Jews that the whole city was in expectation; and the mood seemed to spread out from the city as waves from a stone dropped into a still pond move out toward the shores.

One day about the time of the evening oblation, the guards at the palace challenged a tall, lean, and muscular man—his hairy skin burnt almost black by the sun, his fingernails grown like the claws of a bird, and the hair of his head and his beard grown to his waist. These green recruits had been children when God's judgment fell on Nebuchadnezzar, and they had no idea that this was the mighty king of Babylon. They moved to bar his way, then hesitated and drew back, impressed by the power of his eye and the proud bearing with which he passed them by. The taller of the two guards went hurrying off to find a person of authority to whom he could report this matter.

Meantime, the strange, gaunt figure moved

across the courtyard and passed from room to room. Some, like the guards at the gate, turned as if to inquire his business or command him to leave, but somehow none dared speak. Here and there a courtier who had struck the king to drive him away in the day that the madness fell upon him, now paled at the sight of the king returned and fell to the floor in obeisance crying, "O King, live forever."

Straight to his own apartments went Nebuchadnezzar. They were as he had left them, their royal sanctity preserved by Amytis. For the last several months, clean linens had been placed upon his couch each morning and royal garments draped across the chair. The bare feet, too toughened now to feel the softness of the red and purple carpet, crossed the room to the door of the bath, passed over the blue and crimson tiles, pausing only once as he lifted the hammer from its place to strike a single blow upon the silver gong that called the bath attendants. Now, he plunged into the pool of tepid water, chest deep, relaxing to its embrace, only his head above the surface. Meantime, the bath attendants waited, towels across their arms, the perfumed oil and ointments on a golden tray. The royal barber and long-time confidant of the king, his eyes awash with tears, whetted his razor on the leather strap hanging from his waist while his assistant ran emory stone along the already-sharpened scissors. Finally, the man immersed in the healing waters opened his eyes, his feet now on the bottom of the pool. His mouth, hidden by the overhanging hair of the upper lip and therefore invisible to the watchers in the room, opened to speak. Only a hoarse sound was heard at first. The tongue, these many years unused to human speech, was striving to form the words men understood, the throat to shape the sounds with which men can communicate.

"Blessing and honor and praise to the Most High, the God of heaven, who liveth forever." The words were clear now.

The king moved from the pool to the massage table. Soaped, rinsed, anointed, dried, he gave himself over to the skilled hands of the masseurs, who for an hour or more worked over the muscles, strong as those of a young man. The cuts of thorns and branches, the bruises made by stones and rough walls were anointed with healing medicines. Then the long nails on hands and feet were trimmed. At last, his hair cut again to shoulder length and the beard shaped spade-like, its end barely touching his chest at the base of his throat, he moved again into the bedroom. Here he was clothed in garments that spoke of wealth and power. A servant stooped to place the ankle-high boots on his feet as another approached with rings for his fingers, the gold chain for his neck, and the royal crown, a band of gold with large rough-cut gems marching around its circumference in a procession of rainbow fires. The rings would not fit fingers grown hard and calloused and enlarged, the boots not encompass feet that had walked unbound for seven years. This king whom they feared would lash out in anger only smiled, picked up the signet ring he used to wear upon his first finger and slipped it on the little finger which it fit now and, walking barefoot from the room, traversed the chambers where hundreds were gathered to welcome back their king.

Passing through the prostrate throngs, he reached at last the great throne room where the orchestra, quickly assembled, poured down sweet harmony from their balcony above the door. The crowd that waited there bowed like a field of windswept grain as he passed. The music swelled in volume as he mounted the dais steps, turned, and for a moment stood to survey his subjects, and then took the seat of power to the accompaniment of a final, crashing chord.

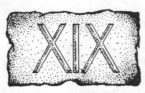 The first official document
to be issued by Nebuchad-
nezzar after his return was
a statement addressed to "all people, nations, and
languages that dwell in all the earth," in which he
set forth the signs and wonders that the High God
had wrought toward him. He gave the account of
his dream and its interpretation, confessed his sins
of pride, and told of the voice from heaven
announcing that the kingdom would be taken
from him and how that judgment fell. He then
recounted how, after the passing of the seven
years, he lifted his eyes toward heaven, and his
understanding returned to him—whereupon he
blessed the Most High and praised and honored
Him who lives forever, whose dominion is an
everlasting dominion, and whose kingdom is from
generation to generation—and how he was
reestablished on his throne and a more excellent
majesty was added unto him. Throughout the
whole document he praised and extolled and
honored the King of heaven, whose works are
truth and who is able to abase those who walk in
pride.

138

Surely no king of any pagan country had ever sent out such a document from one end of his domain to the other. In previous statements, he had threatened to punish those who blasphemed the God of Israel, and he had acknowledged His power to do miracles. In this document, he set down God's dealings with Nebuchadnezzar and his own recognition that these dealings were just and fair. It was at once a confession of sin, an acknowledgment of the righteousness of God's judgment upon that sin, and a personal recognition of the power and greatness of that God.

I am convinced that the "excellent majesty" which the king mentioned as being added unto him was the majesty of humility and faith.

The royal declaration created a tremendous stir throughout the kingdom and throughout all of the neighboring lands. In the city of Babylon alone, there were several thousand who acknowledged that they were fixing their faith in this mighty God whom the king acknowledged. Undoubtedly, some professed conversion in order to please or flatter the king and to gain his favor, but it cannot be denied that many of these professed converts were sincere and genuine. Some sought out teachers among the exiled Jews, asking to be instructed in their faith. Others simply abandoned the temples, removed their household idols, and sought to live pure and honest lives. They addressed their prayers directly to the God whose habitation is on high. Others sought to acquire even the smallest scraps of Scripture, and scribes were kept busy translating the Psalms and other sacred writings into the Aramaic tongue.

All this, of course, stirred the priests of the Chaldean gods into a frenzy of bitterness and hatred. Every sort of scheme was devised to compromise the king or to embarrass him. Dire prophecies of judgments hanging over Babylon were pronounced by Chaldeans and soothsayers, and I sensed now the genuine spirit of unity among the priests of the various gods whose temples were scattered throughout Babylon. There was a definite plan afoot to stir up hatred against the Jews. In spite of all they could do, however, the priests were unable to shake the throne or turn the Babylonians against the great king, who had never before enjoyed such popularity among his people as now.

Crops were abundant, and no shortages were felt throughout the kingdom. The barley, which grew in such abundance in the fertile alluvial soil in all the territory around the city, was producing more than enough to meet the needs of the city and the kingdom. It was being shipped abroad as well.

A little more than five years had passed since his return to sanity when Nebuchadnezzar ended his forty-three-year reign. One morning when his attendants came to wake him, they found him paralyzed, unable to move his right arm or leg, his right eye almost closed, and his mouth drawn down on that side. When the physicians sent for me, I found him surrounded by the members of his immediate family. Nitocris and Amytis were present as were Nabonidus and his wife, the Babylonian princess, and Prince Awil-Marduk. Whether he was aware of their presence, it was impossible to tell, but as far as we could discern, he died quietly without regaining consciousness.

Word of the king's illness had spread through the city, and by noon the processional way was packed with people crowding toward the palace. As governor of the province of Babylon, I went with Awil-Marduk to the battlements over the main entrance, accompanied by Neriglissar and Nabonidus. With us were ensign bearers and a band of trumpeters who played a doleful blast announcing the death of the king. This was followed by a paean in a major key, after which I led Awil-Marduk forward, declaring that according to the will of Nebuchadnezzar, this, his son, was now his father's successor as king of Babylon. This was done immediately following the king's death to settle once and for all any question about who was the legitimate king.

That night, crowned and wearing the royal mantle, Awil-Marduk received the nobles of the realm together with the chief priests, Chaldeans, and wise men in the throne room. Here Awil-Marduk announced thirty days of mourning for the late king, decreeing that no festivals be observed in temples throughout the kingdom during this time.

Unlike the Egyptians, the Babylonians do not practice the art of embalming, and in the heavy, near-tropical climate of Babylon, a dead body begins rapidly to deteriorate and decay. Therefore, early the next morning, Nebuchadnezzar's corpse was cremated in the great open square before the temple of Bel Marduk and the incinerated remains were placed in a glazed jar sealed with the signet of the late king—which was then destroyed—and also with the the signet of the new king, Awil-Marduk. Through the period of official mourning, the urn surrounded with flowers, rested on a high and richly carved stand in the center of the great hall of the palace, four members of the king's own guard standing at attention, one on each side, as the citizens of Babylon—nobles and slaves alike—passed by to pay their tribute to the monarch who had made their city and their kingdom great.

Neither in Babylon nor outside its walls are cemeteries found, save only the Jewish cemetery some distance away. Babylonian kings, unlike the pharaohs of Egypt, do not spend their lives carving mausolea for their remains. It is the custom in Chaldea to entomb the ashes of the dead in their own houses. Sometimes a corner of a room is bricked up, and at times even a small room becomes the receptacle for the ashes and trophies of the dead—the door also being closed up since in this country inner rooms are often without windows or other openings giving directly to the sunshine and fresh air. On occasion, ossuaries are bricked up in the courtyard wall.

When the period of mourning was over, Nebuchadnezzar's ashes were interred in the wall of the second level of the so-called "hanging gardens," a building which is actually a part of the royal palace and a place whose reputation shall live in legend as long as the exploits of Nebuchadnezzar, its royal builder.

 I am afraid in this account I have been so busy dealing with important matters of government and the account of the king that I have neglected to deal with the lives of those who are dear to me.

I suppose as one gets older, he is inclined to think more of the past; for I have found in recent years that my thoughts tend to run back to my boyhood in Jerusalem, and I am wondering whether I shall go back there when the exiles leave Babylon at the end of the seventy years' sojourn that the prophet has indicated is the limit of the captivity.

Also as I grow older, I regret more and more that I never took a wife, and I cannot help envying Belzephon and Rachel, who are still a part of my household. In fact, they are my family. Aside from their daughter, who died in infancy, they have never had children. This I consider sad, indeed, because one of the great comforts of old age is to look upon strong sons and beautiful daughters and rejoice in their children, who are an extension of your own life.

In any case, I tell myself I never found time to marry, kept busy as I was with the affairs of the government. But still, had I as a young man found the right girl, I suppose time would have presented an opportunity for marriage. If Amytis now had been a decade younger and unmarried, she would, I think, have been the woman who most pleased me, having embraced the Jewish faith and embodying as she does those qualities which I most admire.

It is customary in these kingdoms of the East for the queen, upon the death of her husband, to withdraw herself from the public eye even when she is the mother of the reigning monarch. At least it was so in Assyria. I have no doubt that Amytis exercised considerable influence over her son, however. Awil-Marduk, I believe, would have made in time a great man and a strong king. It is hard, however, to walk in the shadow of a man like Nebuchadnezzar, and I know, although I cannot account for the knowledge, that Awil-Marduk has not many months to reign.

Shadrach and Meshach, upon the death of the great king, retired from their positions of leadership and responsibility in the affairs of the city of Babylon, petitioning the young king to replace them with younger men. Now they spend much of their time with the people of the exile and in the study of the Scriptures. Like Belzephon, they are only slightly older than I, which means they are in their early sixties, but—at sixty myself—they seem at least a decade older—

particularly Shadrach, who suffers in this climate from aching in the joints of his hands and knees. It grieves me to see how twisted his hands have become and how large the knuckle joints. I know, though he never mentions it, it causes him great pain to walk any distance, and the stiffness in his limbs is becoming more obvious with the passing of the years.

It seems that the God of heaven preserved Shadrach and Meshach to serve King Nebuchadnezzar. He gave them skill and wisdom in all their doings, but now that Nebuchadnezzar is dead and they have no responsibilities, they have grown suddenly old. I feel, however, almost as young as when I stood before the king to reveal to him his dream of the great image and the interpretation of it. I watch with pride the sons of Abednego, now young men in their prime, and it gives me great joy to employ them on important commissions for the new king.

Queen Amytis comes sometimes to our house to join us in a family meal. Often Shadrach and Meshach are there, as well as Leah, who still keeps house for her sons, worried constantly like every Jewish mother about whom and when they will marry. In fact, I often tease her about wanting to get rid of them so she can sell her house to come and live with us, which is, I know, what she would like to do. All the years have not lessened the close tie of affection that binds those so opposite twin sisters together. As far as Belzephon and I are concerned, she would be most welcome, but I have the feeling that in spite of her deep love for Leah, Rachel would find the presence under her roof of her strong-willed twin something of a burden.

Discreet as she was and a woman who knew how to hold her tongue, Amytis, who was so close to Rachel and who knew that neither Belzephon nor I would ever betray her confidence, spoke quite frankly one evening about the concern she felt. The eunuch and the guards who always accompanied her were having their meal together in the kitchen. We could hear the querulous voice of the eunuch now and then as he complained to our Jewish cook about the quality of Hebrew cooking, which, nonetheless, the cook assured me the eunuch always seemed to enjoy, "if one can judge by the amount he puts down his throat."

Amytis had been quiet and withdrawn all evening until finally Rachel asked her what was wrong. "If it is something you would like to talk about, it might do you good to tell us," Rachel ventured, "and you know it will not pass the walls of this room."

"I hope it is nothing to be concerned about, but I cannot help feeling troubled. My son is about to do something I often begged his father to do, and yet I wish he would not."

"I love paradoxes and contradictions," I said, "but I always wonder, being one man who admits he cannot understand the logic of a woman, why something you have wanted, when it is in your grasp you decide you do not want it at all."

"I am not expressing myself very well, but let

me try to explain," replied the lady. "You and I both wanted Nebuchadnezzar to move the king of Judah and his mother into better quarters than that run-down, little house near Tel-Abib. He ignored requests of mine for a time and when I kept on gave me a very blunt answer that he would not."

I said in agreement, cracking a pistachio nut and dipping it in honey, "Well, if that is what Awil-Marduk is going to do, it seems to me that it would be no source of worry on your part."

"Yes, but it is. He plans to bring Jehoiachin and his mother to live in the palace and eat at the king's table rather than setting them up in a proper house of their own, and for the first time he has given the king's wives permission to come and live with him. You know, I am sure, that all these years they have been confined to a convent of priestesses. Can you imagine these women, no longer young, suddenly released from that strict environment—for these are not priestesses of Ishtar among whom they have lived—and brought into the royal palace with all of its sophisticated courtiers and pompous etiquette?"

"From what Belteshazzar told us, one of them had been married to the young King Jehoiachin only one year and the other wife a year and a half when they were brought to Babylon. They have not been allowed to see him since they came here, have they?" asked Belzephon.

I shook my head in answer. The queen, preoccupied with her problem, returned to that subject. "When she first came here, I felt sorry for Queen Nehushta, captive and living in poverty, and went to see her. That is where I first met you, Belteshazzar, if you remember."

"Oh, I remember well enough," I interjected.

"But I have found that Nehushta is a vicious, long-tongued woman. I still feel sorry for her, but I do not want her in the palace," she continued. "I do not need to tell you, Belteshazzar, who I think knows more than I do about the sentiment here, that the Jews have become something of an issue in Babylon."

Rachel started to speak, but the queen anticipated her remarks. "I know, Rachel, what you are going to say, that many of the Jews have established successful businesses and are competing with the Babylonian merchants, and that has raised jealousies and hatred. Nonetheless, they do exist, whatever the cause."

Here I spoke up to say, "I am afraid sometimes where my people are concerned, there is no cause for these feelings except the gift they seem to have for being abrasive."

"Please, wait a minute," the queen said. "You do not have to defend or explain the Hebrews to me. As a convert, I know our faith itself turns men against us. When we try to be faithful, they think we are proud and regard ourselves as superior. You ran into that when you first came here, Daniel." She called me, as she often did these days, by my Hebrew name. "Well, if we love our God, it is a small price for us to pay in order to obey

Him, but . . ." she broke off.

"You fear that bringing the exiled king to eat at the table of the king of Babylon can become a cause for revolt among the Babylonians, and Awil-Marduk has enemies who would not hesitate to use it."

Belzephon turned to me. "You have spoken of a spirit of revolt, which you are afraid is beginning to grow."

"My son is like his father, hard-headed and determined, but so can I be," said Amytis, frowning in mock fierceness. "I suppose there is nothing I can do to prevent his bringing King Jehoiachin into his household, but I shall see that his mother is left behind—in a better house, of course, but no closer to the palace than Tel-Abib."

Rachel broke in on the silence that followed this remark with her gentle laughter. "This is something I would like very much to see, Your Majesty. I am sure you can work it, but how do you expect to accomplish it?"

"Awil-Marduk is very devoted to his mother, and if I tell him that every time I am around that woman I get a headache, I think his conscience will be inclined to bother him. Besides that, the reigning queen has no more use for that woman than I do, and this is one time that mother-in-law and daughter-in-law will form a firm alliance."

I do not know how Amytis worked it, but when Jehoiachin came to live in the royal palace, his mother remained behind, fretting and fuming and most unhappy in spite of her sumptuous new house and servants in Tel-Abib.

This tenderhearted concern for a captive Judean king spoke much about the nature of Awil-Marduk, who was far too gentle and tender of heart to be king in Babylon, whose greatness had been built on war and conquest by his father. Although Awil-Marduk had taken over the command of the army of the north during his father's madness, he was not loved by the military who always have a tendency to despise gentleness as weakness and even effeminacy. Although still well paid, the soldiers remembered the spoils of battle they had taken across the world; and, sad to say, their fingers itched for blood and pillage.

The priests looked upon the Jews as a threat to their monopolistic religious hold on the hearts and minds of the people. Though there might have been rivalries among the hierarchies of the various gods, the priests recognized the importance of standing together against the threat of a new religion as a common enemy to all. The wise men and the politically ambitious of the Chaldeans have long been jealous of the Jews, whom Nebuchadnezzar appointed to high places in the government—particularly of men like Shadrach, Meshach, Abednego, and me.

Although Hebrews have a reputation across the world of being traders and money-makers— sometimes even unscrupulously and dishonestly— the fact is that Babylon is a city of merchants. Into her walls poured the treasures of Arabia, the riches of India, the dyes of Phoenecia, and the spices of the East. Through her gates caravans of merchandise go out to every corner of the world; and whether going out or coming in, they pile up profit for the people of Babylon. Now here among them, like a canker in their very midst, were these Jews who forty years earlier had been customers for their merchandise and spoils of conquest for their soldiers but who now had become their competitors. The remarkable thing is that there were no bold and open attacks upon the people of the exile. While Nebuchadnezzar lived no one would have dared to instigate such a thing or be a party to it; but there was, nonetheless, a strong sentiment against anything that could advance the welfare of these people at the expense of the prestige and profit of the Babylonians.

Neriglissar, whose hatred for Awil-Marduk I had sensed when we served together on the council of regency during the period of the king's madness, was a strong commander, popular with the army, and a man—it was being whispered in the corners of the streets—who would make a great king.

Merchants and soldiers alike could not talk enough about King Croesus of Lydia, who, according to legend, had sufficient wealth to cover the Greek shrine of Delphi with solid gold. His riches whetted the greed of the soldiers who longed for a king and a general to lead them in a campaign against Croesus and his kingdom.

One moonless night, returning from the temple of Ishtar, Awil-Marduk was murdered in the street near the palace, apparently by men of his own guard who had disappeared. The priests had urged the king to come that night to the temple to observe some strange phenomena in the skies. Since there was no record of any unusual occurrences in the heavens that night, this appears to have been a fabrication of the priests who were in league with some of the army officers to assassinate Awil-Marduk. What happened to the royal guards it is difficult to determine; but the most likely explanation is that they were hidden with their families in one of the temple cloisters until they could be smuggled out of the city; for when, according to Babylonian law, the authorities sought out their families that they might be put to death, none were to be found.

Neriglissar proclaimed himself king, justifying his right to the throne on the basis of his marriage to a daughter of Nebuchadnezzar. If the military had conspired to set him on the throne, Neriglissar proved all that they desired. Cilicia, which had been a Babylonian dependency for almost thirty years, was invaded by Appuashu, the king of the mountainous country to the west. Neriglissar led a well-equipped army to recapture the country. On Neriglissar's approach, Appuashu retired to the foothills, leaving a force to guard the approaches; but the Babylonians crushed these defenses, pushed their way through, and followed him across the rough mountain terrain to his own capital, which they captured and plundered, but they found that Appuashu had fled still further to the island fortress of Pitusue, two miles off shore in the Great Sea. The Babylonian army ravaged the countryside as far as the Lydian border before returning home early the following year.

However much the army may have benefited from the spoils of that expedition, the entire kingdom paid for it by a famine which began almost simultaneously with Neriglissar's assumption of the crown. Where there had been fine crops, there were now only dusty fields. Many died of starvation. Bony hands of gaunt children were outstretched for food on every street corner. Unfortunately, the famine outlasted Neriglissar, continuing altogether for ten consecutive years. The priests, of course, declared this a judgment of the gods for the good treatment which the Jews were receiving; but the fact is, the shortage of food coming on top of the wars and the building activities of Nebuchadnezzar, had produced a cycle of inflation. The level of prices rose by fifty percent during the ten years of the famine and continued to rise rapidly even after the famine had ended with a year of abundant rainfall and bumper crops.

I find that merchants become very reluctant, even when the market is flooded and goods are in abundance, to sell a product for less than they had been able to ask in time of adversity; and even if prices level off, they never seem to decline.

Though not so recognized at the time, an event of tremendous import for the future of Babylon was set in motion while Neriglissar was king: Cyrus became king of Anshan. This gifted and ambitious man was not content with this small kingdom and immediately began to devise means by which he could extend his sway. Within ten years, he had defeated Astyages, king of the Medes, and seized the Median capital Ecbatana. During this time, the friendships and the treaties between Media and Babylon were weakened and eventually ceased to exist.

Meantime, Cyrus had moved against Lydia and conquered it within a year. Croesus, the king of Lydia, had an alliance with Babylon, but Babylon had no time to come to the defense of Lydia so swift had been Cyrus's victory; however, Cyrus realized now that Babylon was an enemy that stood in his way of world domination. A few months of widespread discontent against Neriglissar's rule may have been instigated by Cyrus's agents. The Babylonian king of three years' reign was murdered, and a rival prince took the throne until he too was slain, to be followed by my old friend Nabonidus, husband of the Babylonian princess.

Now sixty years of age, Nabonidus had overcome, I thought, some of the weaknesses and follies of his youth. At least he began well. He made an alliance with Cyrus, hoping thereby to gain the return of Harran to Babylon, this city where his own mother lived, having been captured by the Medes about the time that Neriglissar departed the world.

Nabonidus had sought advice from an oracle of the gods, and it had confirmed that he had nothing to fear from the Medes and that this alliance with Cyrus was most desirable. I did my best to dissuade Nabonidus from this step, warning him that it would prove fatal, but my efforts were of no avail. It was at this time that I asked to be excused from my position in

Babylon. Nabonidus agreed to release me with the understanding that I would occasionally serve him as an ambassador on sensitive missions abroad.

Nabonidus's first military expedition resulted in the recapture of Harran, shortly before his mother, Shamua-Damqa, priestess of Sin, died there at the age of 104.

Perhaps some reader of this journal will in years to come feel that all of this tedious information is an unnecessary hindrance to the flow of the narrative. A hindrance, indeed, it may be, but not an unnecessary one; for it is my purpose here to show how the great God deals in the affairs of nations, and all that I have set down has bearing on the plan of God for the overthrow of Babylon and the return of my people from captivity.

Maybe it was fear of assassination or, perhaps, ambition to prove himself another Nebuchadnezzar by establishing a strong empire and great city of his own that led Nabonidus to attempt to move his capital to Tema in Arabia. In any event, after recovering from an illness in Lebanon and capturing one of the leading towns of Edom, Nabonidus settled in Arabia, making friends of the various tribal leaders and petty kings. He was absent from Babylon for a total of ten years.

Meantime, he had established his son Belshazzar as co-ruler and left him as regent in Babylon. It was in the first year of Belshazzar's reign that I had a very strange and troubling dream in which the four winds of heaven were causing a tumult upon the Great Sea, out of which came strange beasts, each different from the other. The first was a lion with eagle's wings; but as I watched, the wings were plucked, and the lion was lifted up and stood upon its feet as a man. A man's heart was given it. Next came a beast like a bear that raised itself up on one side with three ribs in its mouth between its teeth, to whom someone said, "Arise, devour much flesh." Then I saw another beast like a leopard with four heads and four bird's wings upon its back. Dominion was given to it.

Finally, in my night visions, I saw a fourth beast, very dreadful and terrible to behold and extremely strong, for it had iron teeth; and it devoured and broke in pieces and stamped what was left over with its feet. Unlike any of the other beasts, it had ten horns. As I watched the horns, there came up among them another little horn as three of the first horns were plucked up by the roots; and I saw in this horn eyes like the eyes of a man and a mouth speaking great things. I saw thrones prepared, and the Ancient of Days sat down in garments as white as snow. The hair of His head was like pure wool, and His throne was like a burning flame, His wheels as hot fire. A fiery stream issued before Him, and untold thousands ministered to Him while ten thousand times ten thousand stood before Him. Judgment was set and books were opened. Because of the voice of the great words which the horn spoke, I watched until the beast was slain and his body destroyed and given to burning flame.

For the rest of the beasts, they had their

dominion taken away; yet their lives were prolonged for a while. Then I saw One like the Son of man come with the clouds of heaven. He came to the Ancient of Days and stood near before Him; and to Him was given dominion and glory and a kingdom, that all people, nations, and languages should serve Him. His dominion is an everlasting dominion which shall not pass away, and His kingdom that which shall not be destroyed.

I came to understand the anguish of those who dream terrible dreams which they cannot understand and for which they desire an interpretation. In my vision, I approached one who stood by, and I asked him what all this meant, and he explained it to me: "These great beasts are four kings which shall rise out of the earth. The saints of the Most High shall have the kingdom and will possess that kingdom forever, even for ever and ever." But I still did not understand the thing that troubled me most; so I asked him about the fourth beast. It was different from the others, and I craved especially to know the meaning of the ten horns and of the other horn which came up, before whom three fell away, that horn that had eyes and a mouth, whose appearance was more fearful than the others.

He answered, "The fourth beast shall be the fourth kingdom. It shall be different from the rest of the kingdoms and will devour the whole earth and shall tread it down and break it in pieces. The ten horns are ten kings. Another shall rise after them, different from them; and he shall conquer three kings. He will speak great words against the

Most High and wear out His saints. He shall believe he can change times and laws, and these saints shall be given into his hand until a time and times and the dividing of time; but the judgment shall come, and they shall take away his dominion, to consume and destroy it unto the end. The kingdom and dominion and greatness of the kingdom of the whole earth shall be given to the saints of the Most High, whose kingdom is an everlasting kingdom, and all powers shall serve and obey Him. This is the end of the matter."

The more I thought about this, the more troubled I became. Can it be, I wonder, that what I saw is but another revelation of the great image in Nebuchadnezzar's dream? To him God revealed the future kingdoms as they look to men—important and glorious, seemingly established by men, for they are a part of the form of man. Perhaps God has shown me how these things appear to Him, and I have seen them with the eyes of one of His saints as vicious, devouring, and cruel beasts. To Nebuchadnezzar, the Son of the High God appeared as a great stone for smiting that shall eventually fill the earth, while to me, He was revealed as the Son of man, to whom is given dominion and glory and an everlasting kingdom.

It was two years later that I had another vision. Nabonidus had sent a messenger crediting me as an ambassador to Shushan in the province of Elam, where I was to spend some months as his representative or envoy. Apparently he was still handling the affairs of the kingdom, though at a great distance from the capital, while Belshazzar had only the responsibilities for the affairs of the city itself. However, so weak and lustful and wicked was the son that I was greatly concerned about the condition of the city and its welfare. I was glad, therefore, to get away for a while and leave Babylon.

As I slept in the palace of Shushan, I had a vision in which I was by the bank of the river Ulai, which flows near the city. When the vision had passed and I was trying to ponder its meanings, I saw a man before me and I heard a man's voice between the banks of Ulai say, "Gabriel, make this man to understand the vision"; so he came near where I stood, but as he drew close, I was afraid and fell on my face. He said, "Understand, son of man, for at the time of the end shall be the vision." While he was speaking, I was in a deep sleep on my face upon the ground, but he touched me and sat me up saying, "Behold, I will make you know what shall be in the last time of the indignation, and at the time appointed, the end shall come. The two horns on the ram which you saw are the kings of Media and Persia. The rough goat you saw is the king of Greece, and the great horn that is between his eyes is the first king. That was broken, and four horns stood up in its place; so four kingdoms shall come up out of the nation but without the power of the first kingdom. When the transgressions have gone their full course, a king of fierce countenance who understands obscure sentences shall appear. He shall be mighty in power, but that power is not his own. He shall prosper and do wonderful deeds of destruction. He shall destroy the mighty and the holy people, and through his policy will he cause his schemes to prosper. He shall magnify himself in his heart; and through prosperity shall he destroy many. He also shall stand up against the Prince of princes, but he shall be broken without the power of the hand.

"This vision which you have seen today is true, but keep it to yourself, for it shall be shut up for many days."

I fainted then and was sick for some days, after which I got up and did the king's business, but I could not get over my astonishment at the vision.

I have set down a full account of these visions and their interpretations in the Book which I have written by the Spirit of God. I wonder if all the prophets have been like me, given to see and know things they cannot themselves understand and of which even the interpretation is not clear to them. How much more simple and easy for me to understand were the two dreams of King Nebuchadnezzar for which God gave me the interpretation. I cannot help feeling that much has not been revealed and that there may be great lapses of time between the appearance of the first three kingdoms and the final king; but I am sure of this: someday the kingdom of God's Son will be set up upon this earth, for the words are clear, "it shall fill the whole earth."

I know also that great suffering awaits my people who are God's people in the years and centuries that lie ahead. I can only wonder why God has chosen me to be His messenger; I understand so little of the message myself. The clay of this vessel is too weak to bear the surging revelation of God's secrets of what must yet come to pass. How difficult must it be for the Almighty—and I set down these words with fear and trembling—to strive to reveal His plans for His creation to one of His creatures—incompetent, childlike, and lacking all power to understand. Perhaps what I have written in the Book, which the Spirit of God commanded, will be clear in due season and revealed to the saints as the time of fulfillment draws near, and will be the certainty of their hope and the assurance that His kingdom shall be established and His plan shall be accomplished.

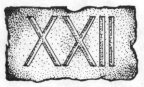When I returned to Babylon on completion of the king's business in Shu-shan, I learned of the death a few days before of Queen Nitocris, the Egyptian widow of Nebuchad-nezzar. Though I had never been as close to her as I was to Queen Amytis, we had known each other, and I had come to have great respect for her unselfishness, her talent, and her wisdom. I went as soon as possible after my return to extend my sympathy to her daughter, the Babylonian princess. It was rumored in court circles that she was the power behind the throne of her son, Belshazzar; and if I had doubted the truth of this speculation, the doubts would have been resolved as the princess and I talked together on the first level of the hanging gardens. I would not imply that she opened her heart to me regarding family affairs or that she discussed the secrets of the government. Her conversation, however, was so open and frank and easy that I could read between the lines things that a stranger might not have seen. I spoke of my admiration for her mother and my sense of loss at her passing, and we talked together

about the gifted lady who had brought her into the world.

"I am so glad you came," she said. "You may not realize this, but of all the people I know in Babylon, your sympathy and understanding mean more to me than that of anyone else, for I know they are genuine and come from the heart. I really came to know you when we worked together during the time of my father's absence."

"Those were difficult days for all of us," I remarked.

"Yes, but you know—and I would not say this to anyone else, for I loved my father dearly—in one way I enjoyed those days. For the first time I felt a sense of freedom and of genuine power, of being able to accomplish something on my own. I do not think I could have enjoyed it had I not believed your assurance that it was only for seven years, for I could not have borne the thought of my father's living out his life like an animal."

"Now," I said, "as queen and mother of a reigning king, you have an opportunity again to embellish Babylon with beautiful buildings and also to lend wise counsel to your son."

"The building—yes, I enjoy that but I think primarily because it takes my mind off the other thing, the weakness which I see. My son has appointed the wrong men to high office. My husband sends us lengthy dispatches, but his mind is on Tema and the new capital he expects to build there. I am afraid he is too old a man for such a project."

"But he is strong and vigorous and always had great dreams," I said.

"Great dreams, yes, but practical ideas—no, I am afraid not. It takes at least one man's lifetime to build a city of greatness and of beauty. A man must be able to inspire fine architects and fire their dreams from his own. He must have loyal subjects as well as a strong body and a gifted mind."

Then, as if drawn by some inward compulsion, she began again to talk about her son. "I would not say this to anyone but you, Belteshazzar. Somehow you draw confidences from me. I sometimes wish Belshazzar were a pious Jew living with his fellows in Tel-Abib or like you, a wise man and a prophet of the High God."

I smiled and expressed my surprise at such a statement.

"No, I mean it," she said. "A faithful Jew following the precepts of his religion is a man at peace. That is something Belshazzar will never be. He is as ambitious as his grandfather, in whose shadow he lives, and as proud as his father, to whom he is answerable, though a king himself."

As if by mutual agreement, we changed the subject and began to talk of her plans for a new type of warship. Nothing was said, of course, of Belshazzar's well-known dissipation, which was the subject of much of the gossip of the city, but we talked of trivial things.

Twice I rose to go, and twice she urged me stay awhile. The sun was almost hidden behind the western wall when at last I took my leave.

"Though you pretend to live in retirement," she said, "I know of the ways in which you serve my husband, and I thank you. By the way, your twin nephews are much like their uncle. You can be proud of them."

I knew she was speaking of Azariah's sons and did not feel led to disabuse her regarding the relationship; for, after all, their grandfather had been a second cousin to my mother.

A few days later, I returned to the palace to pay my respects to another queen. Amytis had sent a very strange message asking me to come to see her, saying it was important that we not put off the visit. I found her propped up with cushions upon a bench in the inner private courtyard just off her apartment. I had never been in this part of the palace before and wondered why she chose this time to have me brought here, but as I bowed to kiss her hand, I felt the heat of her palm and looked up into eyes that were bright and feverish, sunk in dark circles in the gentle face of an old lady crowned with white hair. Although well past eighty now, she had always—even the last time I had seen her—seemed so very young, her spirits soaring, her voice lilting and melodious, her laughter the laughter of a girl. I sensed the pain within the form now grown so fragile and saw it now and again pass across her eyes, but for the most part she managed to keep it very well hidden.

She smiled and teased me saying, "I hear you

saw the young queen the other day, but your old friend had to send for you. I am glad you came back from Shushan when you did, or we might never have met again in this life."

I explained to her the reason for my visit to Nitocris and told her I had planned to come to see her very soon. I asked her how she was feeling and if she knew the nature of her illness. We were too honest with each other for me to have said, "I am sure it is nothing. You will be better soon," for we both knew her time was very short.

"I want you to promise me something," she said.

I took her hand and answered, "I will."

"I do not want to be cremated and stuck into a corner of a room or placed like a memorial tablet in a wall somewhere. I want to be buried as a child of faith, laid to rest in the good earth to feed the worms and wait the resurrection. Like the wise man you have told me of, I know that when worms have destroyed this body, still in my flesh I shall see God."

"You want me to see that you are buried in the Jewish cemetery?"

"That is it, and you promised."

"It will not be an easy matter to arrange," I said. "There must be for a queen of Nebuchadnezzar a public cremation."

"I think not," she replied. "My slaves I freed a long time ago. My only attendants are Jewish ladies from good families, and my one eunuch came here among the captives also. The queen mother, the Babylonian princess, has agreed to handle this matter with her son, if necessary. In this palace there are so many people that death is not an infrequent visitor. I will have my ladies prepare me for burial. The eunuch will bring the porters to convey me outside the wall and place my remains on a barge."

I could think of many objections to the scheme but ventured only one. "But the men who bring you out will know who it is they are carrying."

She shook her head and smiled. "Do not worry about that; just promise me that you will be on the barge and will supervise the burial."

"Yes, of course I will but—"

She interrupted, "Now, let us talk of other things."

She asked me to hand her from the table a glass of wine in which was a pain-killing drug. As I handed it to her, I protested that it was time I left so she could rest.

"No," she said, "this is our last time to talk. Stay awhile. Let us talk of days gone by. While I was sitting here in the shade before you came, it just occurred to me that you were the only man of whom Nebuchadnezzar was afraid."

"Afraid?" I laughed. "Nebuchadnezzar never feared any man. Why should he be afraid of a Jewish servant, for that is what I was to the king?"

"Why do you think he did not command your presence for the adoration of the great golden image, why he avoided you so long after that fiasco when he was sure you could have interpreted his dream at the first?"

"I thought that was a royal whim, anger perhaps."

"It was a guilty conscience," smiled Amytis. "He feared your God. He knew you never hesitated to speak truth. He was ashamed and dreaded your disapproval. He used to say of you, 'He is the one absolutely honest man in my kingdom.' "

Two nights later the gentle queen died shortly before morning. There were no problems. Her ladies prepared the body and placed it in the room that one of them occupied; and those who took the body away believed it to be one of the Jewish exiles. It never occurred to them that they were bearing the body of the queen. As they were leaving the palace, a guard at the gate said, "Who is it this time?" The eunuch replied, "Only a woman of the Jewish faith."

No one sent me word of Amytis's death, but I awakened before dawn, knowing that she was dead. I dressed hurriedly and was at the barge when they brought her on board. Abednego's twin sons came to the dock just as we were about to cast off for the trip down the river. Although no one had notified them, they each had with him a tool for digging, and it was they who prepared the grave.

We laid her to rest among the daughters of Zion who had hung their harps on the willow trees unwilling to sing the songs of their homeland in the shadows of the walls of Babylon.

No public announcement was ever made of her

death. In fact, so seldom did she appear in public that she was not missed for several weeks. Somehow his mother settled the matter with Belshazzar, who had always resented the fact that one of his grandfather's wives had been converted to the faith of a defeated and exiled people; however, he did have the grace to order a memorial stone and visit the grave when it was put in place. For a long time after, when anyone inquired about Queen Amytis, the answer was a raised eyebrow and the question, "Did you not know? She embraced the Hebrew faith"; and nothing more was said.

 Although I was now officially retired as governor over the affairs of Babylon, old friends who were still in office often came to ask my advice about some problem facing them, and not a week passed but I was visited by some friends among the exiles. Perhaps it was the vanity of old age, but I was particularly pleased that the young men—the sons and grandsons of the elders, among them those who had followed the wanderings of Nebuchadnezzar's madness—came as often as did their fathers; and sometimes I felt like a veritable patriarch of a tribe. I often heard more court gossip and learned more facts about the government from my countrymen than I did from the governors and princes of the kingdom. These exiles seemed to know everything that went on in secret and, being wise, discussed it only among themselves, seeming to the Babylonians to be ignorant and disinterested in what was occurring in the palace and among the great ones of the land.

It was from Abonizah, both an Hebrew and an official in the government of Babylon, that I heard of an incident that gave me cause for alarm.

Belshazzar the king went on a lion hunt accompanied by his usual retinue for such an occasion and taking with him also several young men who were his special friends, among them Mardonius, the son of Gubaru. The king and Mardonius were separated from the rest of the party when a fierce lion sprang to attack them. Instead of holding his ground beside Mardonius and raising his spear to meet the lion's charge, Belshazzar turned and ran, leaving Mardonius to face the lion alone.

By the time the huntsmen who had seen this from a distance could reach the place, Mardonius had been so mangled and torn by the beast that he died. Foolishly the king, instead of permitting the body to be carried home for a proper and honorable cremation, had it taken to one of the places of cremation outside the city where the bodies of the common people were given to the flames; so along with the news of his son's death, Gubaru received from the king's hand a vessel containing his ashes. The father, grieved for his firstborn son, insulted by the manner of his cremation, and angered at the king's cowardice, swore to be revenged on Belshazzar and immediately left Babylon, going to offer his service and experience as a soldier to King Cyrus.

Because King Nabonidus had been now some years out of Babylon, the new year festival in which the king went through the ceremony of taking Marduk's hand was not celebrated although Belshazzar tried to force the priests to let him perform the rite in his father's behalf. Their refusal incensed Belshazzar, and the threats he made in private against the priests were, of course, reported to them almost before they had passed the king's lips, thus widening the breach between the king and these influential ecclesiastics. The result was the priests got into communication with Gubaru, plotting with him to overthrow the dynasty and destroy both Belshazzar and Nabonidus, his father, provided he could be somehow brought back to Babylon—a thing that seemed impossible to accomplish since he had not even returned to the city for the elaborate mourning ceremonies that followed upon his mother's death some years before.

Meantime, King Cyrus, having defeated Croesus, was pressing an even more intense propaganda campaign, winning over local priests and princes throughout the provincial cities of the kingdom on the pretext that he would free them from Babylonian tyranny. Syria and the lands along the eastern shore of the Great Sea were separated from Babylonian control with hardly a battle, Belshazzar making no effort to hold this area for his father who was busy in the South.

When Nabonidus finally returned after an absence of so many years, it was because Cyrus—now called the king of Persia—had extended his power over the entire northern frontier of Babylonia and had begun to march in the direction of Babylon itself. Because Cyrus had also won over to his support the sheiks and petty kings of the desert areas toward Tema, Nabonidus was forced out of his new capital, and there was nothing he could do except abandon it and head at top speed for Babylon.

The new western empire which he had set out to establish collapsed without a struggle, and it seemed likely that Babylon would also. Spies and traitors within the city were undermining whatever confidence was left in Belshazzar and Nabonidus, and Cyrus was being represented as a liberal and tolerant administrator who would free what was left of Babylonia from the tyranny of Belshazzar and Nabonidus.

The land was in the grip of a new famine. The sea peoples along the Persian Gulf coast were in revolt, and the armies of Cyrus were ready for their assault upon the city. In spite of all his follies and weaknesses, Nabonidus was no coward and marched northward to meet the army of Cyrus at the Median Wall, hoping to turn aside or destroy the Persian army before they could reach the city.

Meantime, Belshazzar, hated by the populace and without having made proper arrangements for the provisioning of the city, was in the midst of a land smitten with famine, threatened by invading armies, and riddled with treason. He continued to give himself over to a course of drunkenness and debauchery, which had come to dominate more and more this weak and effeminate man.

 All around the city hunger walked the streets, but inside the palace walls there was abundance. The huge kitchens had been busy for a full day roasting whole lambs and oxen over the firepits on great iron grills. Every sort of rare bird had been prepared—peacocks dressed in their own skins, their feathers intact and the tail plumage spread out like great fans, set out on silver dishes; roast pigeons stuffed with rice; birds, swans, ducks, and geese roasted whole or baked in pastries. There were large fish from the Persian Gulf swimming on a green sea of gelatinous pudding. Pervading the area of the palace near the kitchens was a fragrant smell of roasting almonds and spices where the pastry cooks were concocting honeyed delights sprinkled with raisins. Servants were filling ornate gold and silver pitchers from wineskins hanging on hooks along the wall.

The guests began to gather before sundown in palace courtyards and anterooms where they were handed cups of wine by attentive slaves. As dusk fell, lamps were lighted just as a trumpet note announced the arrival of the king in the banquet hall. The great doors swung open as the guests entered, bowed to the king, and took their seats upon cushions around the low tables scattered throughout the great room where they were given cool cloths perfumed with attar of roses with which to refresh themselves by wiping their faces and hands. The king sat at a similar, somewhat larger table upon a raised dais in the very center of the room so that all the guests could feel near to the royal person and none be more honored than another. The great square chamber, 200 paces in length and width, had a lofty ceiling of Lebanon cedar, the beams resting upon massive columns of glazed brick laid in intricate patterns. Doorways, twice the height of a tall man, in opposite walls gave easy access on one side to the guests and on the other to the slaves bringing food and drink from the kitchens under the direction and supervision of efficient eunuchs, who saw to it that no guest was neglected and no table overlooked.

The female slaves had been carefully chosen for the occasion, all of them graceful and attractive with these attractions well displayed beneath the single, nearly transparent garment each wore, girded at the waist with a colored sash. The men servants were entirely naked save for loincloths and girdles and collars after the Egyptian style.

Tall lampstands with hanging oil lamps were placed around the bases of the columns and along the walls on either side. Still others hung on chains from the lofty ceiling between the columns, the highly glazed brick which covered the walls to the height of the doors reflecting the brilliance of the lamps and giving an illusion of even greater light. The intricate designs of the cornice painted on the plastered walls above the brick seemed to the gaze of the tipsy guests to move and sway in rhythm with the music of the orchestra from the balcony, music that could scarce be heard above the raised voices and raucous laughter of feasters growing increasingly drunk with every passing hour. In Babylon a royal banquet lasted for hours on end. The courses did not follow immediately the one upon the other. Between each course was time for entertainment and for drinking and even for religious festivities, hymns and praise to the gods of Babylon. Dancers gyrated between the tables, stepping lightly over the forms of snoring guests who, overcome with the warmth of the room and the effects of the wine, were dozing now half on and half off the cushions where they sat to feast.

After about four hours Belshazzar, drunk as much with pride as with wine, conceived the idea of sending for the golden vessels of the Temple at Jerusalem that he and his guests might drink from them while they praised their Babylonian gods. Even in the height of his pride before madness overtook him, this was something that Nebuchadnezzar would never have dared to do; and this act of blasphemy was the deathblow of the Babylonian empire.

Suddenly upon the plastered wall just above a massive bronze lampstand appeared the fingers of a man's hand—not the entire hand but just the fingers—holding a stylus and writing in flaming letters four words. Now Belshazzar's countenance, once red with wine, became like that of a dead man—pale and green in color. He was hardly able to raise himself from the cushions where he sat, his legs weak and his knees trembling with terror. The streams of moisture that ran down his face and neck were not mere perspiration from the warmth of this windowless room but the sweat of dread and fear. He cried to his eunuchs and his servants and his pages to bring in the astrologers, Chaldeans, and soothsayers. The golden vessel of the Temple from which he had been drinking lay now forgotten on the floor, the dregs of wine poured out like blood upon the pavement.

Meanwhile, the guests to whom the writing on the wall was visible spoke in hushed tones, glancing uneasily from the king to the flaming words. Others, seated where the columns obscured their vision, moved to behold what it was that entranced the gaze of those around the king. Little by little, the loud voices quieted, and the laughter was hushed. The orchestra had ceased to play, and only the snores of sleepers broke the eerie silence in the room as the wise men and soothsayers and Chaldeans entered to prostrate themselves before the frightened sovereign.

Pointing with a trembling hand to the words upon the wall, Belshazzar cried, "Whichever one of you can read this writing and interpret it for me shall be dressed in royal scarlet with a chain of gold about his neck and be made the third ruler in this kingdom."

They gazed upon the symbols above the candlestick, stroking their beards or shaking their heads in wonder. A few whispered together, but finally they could only confess their inability to read the writing or interpret it. Belshazzar seemed more terrified than ever—if that were possible—by their failure to interpret and explain it.

It was at this moment that his mother, Nitocris called the Babylonian princess, entered the room to stand behind her trembling son, her hand upon his shoulder as she gazed with him at the writing on the wall. A frightened eunuch had come to wake her from her sleep, urging her presence in the banquet hall. Nitocris, unable to understand from the terrified eunuch exactly what had occurred, had dressed hastily and hurried to see for herself. Though frightened, she was too much the queen to show it. She stood now in the grip of conflicting emotions—embarrassment for the weakness Belshazzar her son was displaying, concern for the welfare of the kingdom, curiosity as to what this might portend, and concern to bring some order out of the chaos in this room.

In an effort to lend some dignity to this frightened man, she spoke the formal words of address in a voice loud enough to be heard to the end of the hall, "O King, live forever"; then bending close, she whispered in his ear, "Do not let your thoughts disturb you. Remember you are a king. Control yourself. You are as pale as a dead man and trembling like a reed in the wind. Shame on you."

Then raising her voice again and standing fully erect, she said, "There is a man in this kingdom in whom is the spirit of the holy gods. Light and understanding and wisdom, like the wisdom of the gods themselves, were found in this man whom King Nebuchadnezzar, your father, put in charge of all the magicians, astrologers, Chaldeans, and soothsayers. Let this man Daniel be called, whom the king named Belteshazzar. He can show you what this writing means. He has an excellent spirit and knowledge and understanding. He can interpret dreams and reveal obscure sentences. He knows how to dissolve doubts."

"But all the wise men and magicians and Chaldeans were not able to explain it," Belshazzar sighed, hopeless in his fear.

"Let Daniel be called, and he will interpret this," his mother repeated, digging her fingers into his shoulder blades in her insistence.

The king, now somewhat in control of himself, turned to a soldier, one of the few men in the room entirely sober, saying, "Go fetch Daniel here at once."

It was about four hours before daylight when one of my servants woke me with the announcement that the king commanded my presence immediately at the palace, and his messenger awaited to escort me. Though Belshazzar had seen me around the palace often enough when he was a child and a young man, I had never spoken to him, but he could not have failed to have heard my name mentioned or know something of my relation to the king, his grandfather. So I inquired of the soldier the reason of this summons now in such haste in the middle of the night, and by the time we entered the banquet room, I knew of the king's blasphemy and desecration of the Temple vessels and the writing above the lampstand.

His first words, shouted down the hall as I entered the distant door, were, "Are you Daniel of the children of the captivity of Judah, one of those my father brought out of Judea?"

"I am, O King," I said, making my way between the tables toward the dais. Now I stood before him clearly revealed in the light of the lamp that hung above the table.

"I have heard of you that the spirit of the gods is in you and that light and understanding and wisdom are present."

He explained how the wise men and the soothsayers were unable to interpret the meaning of the writing and urged me to tell him what it meant, promising if I could do so that I would be clothed in scarlet with a chain of gold and be named the third ruler in the kingdom.

Speaking so that all could hear, I answered, "Let the king give his rewards to someone else and keep his gifts, but I will read the writing unto the king and interpret it for him. The Most High God gave Nebuchadnezzar, your father, a kingdom of majesty and glory and honor so that all nations and peoples trembled and feared him. He destroyed those whom he wished to destroy, and he spared the lives of those whom he wished to spare. He set men up, and he debased men according to his whim; but when his heart became vain and his mind was hardened by pride, he was deposed from his royal throne, and his glory was taken away. He was driven out from among men, and he had a heart like a beast. He dwelt with wild asses, and they fed him grass like an ox. His body was wet with the dew of heaven until he recognized the fact that the Most High God ruled in the kingdom of men and that He appoints over it whomsoever He will."

I referred to Nebuchadnezzar as his father in the formal sense of forefather or ancestor after the fashion of this land. "But you, Belshazzar, have not humbled your heart, though you knew all this. You have, moreover, raised up yourself against the Lord of heaven. You have brought here the vessels of God's house and, with your lords and your wives and your concubines, have drunk wine in them, perverting and debasing that which is sacred while you praise gods of silver and of gold and of brass and of iron and of wood and stone, which cannot see nor hear; and the God in whose hand your breath is and who gives you the direction of life, you have not glorified.

"For this reason, the part of the hand was sent from God and this writing was written. *Mene*: God has numbered your kingdom and finished it. *Tekel*: You are weighed in the balances and found lacking. *Peres*: Your kingdom is divided and given to the Medes and Persians."

Proud and dissolute though he may have been, Belshazzar was like his grandfather Nebuchadnezzar, an honorable man who fulfilled his commitments. Many a tyrant would have ordered killed on the spot a messenger of ill tidings, but Belshazzar commanded that I be dressed in a scarlet robe of authority, and he put a chain of gold around my neck and made a proclamation that I should be the third ruler in the kingdom. I bowed and left the room, almost slipping in the spilled food and wine on the floor.

As I went through the anteroom, I heard a clanging of weapons and the rattle of armor and found myself face to face with Gubaru, clothed as he had appeared to me that day in my house in the armor of a Persian general, the broad, short sword in his hand, and the helmet of a commander upon his head. Now behind him Persian soldiers filled the room as I greeted him by name, asking what he was doing here, though I knew well the answer.

"Ridding Babylon of wickedness and tyranny," he answered. "Do not be concerned, my friend. Only those of the blood of Nabonidus need fear the Persians or the power of Cyrus, the great king, whose commander I am."

Followed by his men, he entered the banquet hall. As I came out of the palace, I found Persian soldiers were everywhere. I did not doubt that the area was completely occupied by the enemy; but no man raised a hand to stop me as I passed through the gates and returned home.

The Persians, just out of the view of watchers on the walls of Babylon, had diverted the Euphrates back to its original course, turning it around the city and thus leaving the empty riverbed beneath the watergates a means of ingress to the city; and through this muddy avenue, the force of the Persians moved to occupy in one night a large part of great Babylon.

Only Belshazzar was slain. A short time later Nabonidus, his father, was killed when the army surrendered after being surrounded near the Median Wall by the army of Cyrus.

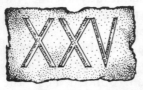

So it happened that in one night the mighty kingdom of Babylon ceased to exist, and the great city was no longer an important world capital but, incorporated into the expanding Medo-Persian empire, it was now only the capital of what had been the province of Babylon. This was accomplished with the death of two men—Nabonidus and his son Belshazzar.

When most important empires come to an end, thousands die or are led captive, cities are leveled, and all is changed. It was not so in Babylon, and the average man who dwelt within the walls of the city might have known no more than that the palace of its king was now occupied by the representative of a new dynasty and that certain processes and departments of the government were being reorganized. Only after some months would he be aware that he was now living under the laws of the Medes and Persians—laws more strict and inflexible than had ever existed within the city before. Formerly the king could set a law aside on a whim and establish a new law with a word. It was different with the laws of the Medes and Persians which, once enacted, could not be removed and were as inflexible as the laws of nature and the rules of the universe itself.

Instead of immediately setting up his capital in Babylon, Cyrus, who never liked the hot and sultry climate there, appointed Gubaru to rule the city and province of Babylon for him. To make it clear to all that he was serving the great Cyrus, Gubaru selected the royal name of Darius, which is, indeed, not a name so much as a title like Pharaoh, which has been applied to the Egyptian rulers for centuries. Just how much responsibility for the reorganization of the government Cyrus left upon the shoulders of Darius, I cannot say. Both were military men, but Cyrus was an experienced ruler as well; so I would be surprised if Darius did not rely heavily upon the great emperor for guidance in the program. Whoever devised it, it was far more effective a system than that under Nebuchadnezzar, though it was, of course, more limited in scope since it was applied now to a single province and not to the widespread kingdom of Nebuchadnezzar.

The kingdom, formerly the province of Babylon, was divided now into 120 smaller territories and a prince appointed to govern each. Over these he appointed three presidents to whom the princes were accountable, and Darius, to my great surprise, appointed me to be the first of the presidents. So instead of being the third ruler of the kingdom as Belshazzar had nominated me a few moments before his death, I was now the second ruler of Babylon.

When Darius summoned me to the palace to tell me of my appointment, I made bold to protest that at my age I was hardly qualified for such a position, as I had now passed my eightieth birthday.

"Your mind is keener than many men I know who are half your age. You are experienced, respected, and trusted. Since you have sought to stay out of the limelight these last few years, you will not be identified in the minds of the people of Babylon with Nabonidus and Belshazzar. Your responsibilities under Nebuchadnezzar and the wisdom with which you discharged them are legendary in this city, and your interpretation of the writing on the wall is a source of conversation in every tavern and street corner."

"It pleases the king to be gracious and flatter me beyond my deserts; but I am a Jew, and there are many in this city who dislike our race and are suspicious of all Hebrews," I reminded Darius. "One of the men whom you have appointed to be a president is a man I had to rebuke and discipline because of his disloyalty to Nebuchadnezzar. He will find it very difficult to work under me."

"He will, nevertheless, work under you or be removed from the presidency," replied Darius. "So we will consider the matter of your appointment a settled thing."

I will not pretend that I was not glad to be busy again serving under a king I admired, a fair-minded and honorable man. Most of those who had been appointed by Darius treated me with respect and seemed willing, for the most part, to accept my suggestions and recommendations. Nergal-Iddin and Charezer, the other two presidents, were a different matter altogether. Charezer never bothered to disguise his dislike for me and when the three presidents met together did not hesitate to speak out in opposition to any position I took. He had never forgiven me for having removed him from his office of chief tax collector in the time of Nebuchadnezzar when he proved himself a venal man, greedy for bribes. I was confident he had not changed; but because he knew I was checking up on him very carefully now, he was limited in his ability to skim off very much for himself.

Nergal-Iddin was entirely different in his manner—so suave and full of flattery that I was sure he could not be trusted; and, indeed, as later events proved, he was entirely different from what he pretended to be. Some time later I learned that these two were conspiring my overthrow so they could have a free hand in their thievery and knavery, and they planned to introduce the same system of pay-off for favors that prevailed generally throughout the Persian empire but which I would not tolerate in Babylon. I found out that they had actually approached some of the men who were close to me in an attempt to bribe them to spy on my doings and see if they could find some evidence of corruption or malfeasance in office in order to bring me down.

Finally, in frustration, they decided that the

only thing they could use against me was my religious practice as a Jew. They went to Darius pretending to represent me as well as themselves and saying that all the presidents were agreed that a decree be issued declaring that for thirty days anyone who prayed to any god except the king was to be thrown into the lions' den. Darius, a relatively frank and open man and still somewhat inexperienced in government, issued the decree. He found the suggestion flattering and was undoubtedly influenced by these two suave liars but took hold of the idea as a means to rally the province in loyalty to its sovereign and strengthen his influence with the people.

Had Darius given more thought to the matter, he would have realized that his decree could cause great resentment among the priests, still a large and influential part of the population. He had, in effect, declared that no ceremonies could take place at any of the temples throughout the kingdom and no sacrifices could be made since petitions to the gods were a part of all such ceremonies. Priests would be denied the offerings from their worshippers and their profit from the sale of religious items and incense and sacrificial animals. This decree effectively closed every temple in Babylon for thirty days. Politically, it was a very unwise move on the part of the king and was deeply resented by a large part of the citizenry—particularly the women who found an emotional outlet in their daily visits to the shrine of their favorite god and those lewd men who engaged in the orgiastic worship of Ishtar.

I was unaware of all this until the night before the decree was to go into effect. It did not take me long to realize who had instigated it or to recognize the motives. I was sure when Darius understood the effect it would have upon all the priests and religious authorities of the realm, he would be extremely angry and upset. In some respects, kings are much like the rest of us. They do not like being made a fool of, and in their royal pride their resentment is perhaps greater than that of other men as is their power to revenge themselves upon those who scheme to put them in an embarrassing and untenable position.

In all the years since I had passed my examinations and left the house of princes, I had made it a habit to pray three times a day with my window open to Jerusalem. While I was a student, my days were so occupied that I was not free to set aside a time of prayer during the day itself but had to confine my devotions to morning and evening, before and after the time of my studies. Now my time was my own, to spend as I wished so long as I did not neglect my responsibilities to the king.

I knew that I would be too old to return with the exiles at the end of the captivity, but my heart still grew warm with thoughts of the Holy City, and my prayers were always for the peace of Jerusalem and the welfare of my people; so I had grown accustomed to praying toward the place where the altar of my God had been set up and the mountain of His tabernacle. My window toward Jerusalem opened onto the courtyard and garden of the house, not toward the public street, and could not be readily observed by passersby; so it was with no thought of being seen in prayer that I had selected the window ledge upon which to rest my elbows while making my petitions known to heaven. I could not now, however, pray in some other place or close the westward windows of my chamber without seeming to deny my God and compromise my faith. This I had never done in all my life, and I was not going to be guilty of it now when an old man.

Nergal-Iddin and Charezer were too eager for my overthrow to merely set spies to watch me but went themselves with witnesses, having rented a house across the street, from the second floor of which they could observe my window. When they saw me at prayer, they hurried off, of course, to let Darius know of it, first reminding him of his decree which, under the laws of the Medes and Persians, could not be set aside, and then letting him know that I was guilty of its violation.

Darius was furious and immediately saw through the whole scheme. He was not angry with me but rather respected me for my consistency. He was angry with himself for not having stopped to think that the decree he had been induced to pass was one that I would certainly be compelled to disregard because of that consistency. In the months since he had taken the throne, he had come to rely upon me, and the affection we had felt for each other over the years had grown stronger in these last months. He had, moreover, just been studying the reports which I had forwarded to him regarding Charezer and Nergal-Iddin and was on the very point of replacing them with other men more trustworthy.

He spent the day trying to devise some means of setting the decree aside or some basis on which he could pardon my offense. He even consulted with me in the matter.

"Can't you, Belteshazzar, who know the law, find some device by which we can get around it? There must surely be some loophole," he entreated. But I could only remind him of the inflexibility of the Persian law which bound king and commoner alike.

Darius delayed as long as possible, and when I had not been sent to the lions' den at sundown, my enemies came again to Darius, demanding that he obey his law. It was full dark, therefore, before they brought me to the mouth of the den. The king himself was there, assuring me, "Your God whom you serve continually will deliver you."

This lions' den itself was under the Ishtar Gate with a wide opening on either side into the area between the first and the second walls of the city. The beasts were able, therefore, to pace up and down in the open air or withdraw into the great cave-like area under the roadway itself. There was a gate in the inner wall behind the hanging gardens, which gave way to a passage terminating in a heavy grilled gate above the den itself. Inside this gate was an open platform and steep steps which led down to the deep cave-like cellar.

Criminals condemned to die were normally thrown off the platform. In my case, however, the king had the gate opened, and I walked through and descended the stairs from the platform. The gate was locked, and my enemies had the effrontery to demand that a stone with the royal seal be placed outside the grill, implying that the king might make some effort to rescue me. They insisted, therefore, that the stone slab be sealed with Darius's seal and with theirs also.

As I descended the steps, I was conscious of the shapes moving shadowlike in the light of the full moon that shone in from the area between the city walls; and as I came toward the bottom of the stairs, I was very aware of the musty and fetid smell of the beasts. Then I saw the figure of a man who stepped out of the shadows to meet me as I reached the floor of the den. I did not need to ask who he was or why he was here. I could not see his face in the darkness of the place, silhouetted as he was against the moonlight of the entrance, and I said to him, "For the first time in all these years, I meet you face to face, and it is too dark for me to discern your features or tell what you look like."

"You saw me for a moment when I stood between you and the wrath of the king," he replied.

"Yes, but only your broad-shouldered back. And I have seen you in the edge of my visions many times. Go with me out into the moonlight so I can have a good look at you."

Turning he took me by the hand, and we walked out of the den between the quiet lions.

"Look closely," said the angel, "so you will recognize me when I come to escort you into the presence of the Great King, before whom the kings of the earth are but as grasshoppers."

His was a face I had seen in my visions when an angel spoke—the same high forehead, wise and gentle eyes, the straight nose, the strong chin, and the crowning curls the color of the gold dust on the jeweler's worktable. He wore a breastplate of shining metal that seemed in the moonlight to change like the changing colors of a sunset sky.

"So this is how you look," I said.

"Sometimes," he answered.

"You mean you are not always the same?" I asked.

He seemed to change the subject. "Do you remember when you were first learning to ride a horse? One day near Bethlehem, the mare on which you rode was frightened by a snake and ran away."

It was an incident I had never forgotten. "Of course," I said. "I tried to rein her in but could not hold her. If it had not been for the shepherd standing by the mouth of the cave who caught her by the bridle, I might have been thrown," I said.

"Do you not recognize the shepherd?"

As I looked, he seemed to change; and there before me was the man who had stopped my horse those seventy years ago.

"So that was you."

"Oh, we have met face to face more than once, and we shall meet again, for I have been assigned from the moment of your birth until the end to be your guardian and your champion, wise man, who knows so many things but not how to defend yourself."

"Perhaps because you have always been there, I never needed to learn self-defense."

A lion stirred restlessly, growling in his throat. The angel spoke a word I could not understand, and the great beast lowered his head upon his paws, watching us with eyes that glowed catlike in the half-dark where a shadow fell across the ground.

"You are not afraid," the angel said. It was a statement, not a question.

"Need I be?" I answered.

"Their mouths are shut. They cannot even yawn," replied my heavenly friend. "Come, let us walk among them."

As we moved through the recumbent forms, I thought what wonderful beasts these are; and turning to the angel I asked, "Did you behold these lions in that eastward garden where Adam and Eve walked in the eveningtime with God?"

"They were like kittens then," and for the first time I saw traces of a smile upon his face; then his brow was sad. "Look at that young lioness. See, she has just dropped her first cub and how she labors trying to give birth to the second. She is too young, the cub within too large and badly placed. She will be dead by morning."

"Can you not help her?" I asked.

The angel shook his head. "I am here in your behalf. I have no power or dominion over beasts," he said, "except to close their mouths and chain their savage natures for this night."

"But look how that tiny, feeble cub tries to find the source of food." I stooped and lifted up the little creature and set him against his mother's belly where he nuzzled until he found the teat and began to pull hungrily upon it.

"Take him with you when you go out tomorrow. He will remind you of this night. He has never tasted human flesh and never shall. See that old lion there?" he said. "Go, rest your head upon his neck, and sleep awhile. It is not long until morning, and your eyes are heavy now."

I did as I was told. It seemed I hardly pillowed myself upon the great beast than the first rays of the sun reflected in the patch of sky above the lofty city walls whose tops towered over us like cliffs above a narrow chasm. But it was the voice of Darius that awoke me, calling through the iron bars of the gate, "Daniel, Daniel, servant of the living God. Is your God, whom you serve continually, able to spare you from the lions?"

As I started toward the stairs, I turned to thank my angelic companion. He pointed to the lion cub sleeping beside its dead mother. "Take him, Daniel. You and I still have much time together. I will stay here to restrain the beasts until you are through the gate. They can still behold me, though you will not."

Turning now from picking up the cub, I found my guardian had vanished from my sight. Mounting the stairs, I cried, "O King, live forever, my God has sent His angel to shut the lions' mouths. They have not hurt me, because before Him He found me innocent, and also before you, my king, have I done no evil."

The king commanded that the gate be opened, and I walked free, a sleeping cub against my breast. The king searched me for any sign of scratch or toothmark, marveling at the power of my God to keep me safe.

"May it please you, my sovereign, that I have this cub whose mother died during the night and who cannot live there in the den?"

"Only if you name him Gubaru," Darius replied.

Commanding me to remain where I was, Darius had the two presidents, their wives, and children brought down and cast from the platform into the lions' den. So hungry were the beasts that they seemed to catch them before they struck the floor, breaking their limbs and tearing flesh from bone as I turned my back in horror from the scene.

Later that day Darius sent a decree through all his realm, addressing it to people, languages, and nations that dwell in all the earth, wishing them peace and commanding that in every dominion of his kingdom men should tremble and fear before the God of Daniel, for He is a living God and steadfast forever and His kingdom one which shall not be destroyed and His dominion one which shall last forever, concluding with these words: "He delivers and rescues, and He works signs and wonders in heaven and in earth, this God who has delivered Daniel from the power of the lions."

So God prospered me through the reign of Darius and even after he had been replaced by Cyrus some time later.

Gubaru the lion cub was put to nurse at one of the great hunting mastiffs who had lost her single pup at birth. At first we muzzled her, afraid of her reaction to the smell of the lion and fearing she might harm him, but her maternal nature accepted him readily, and she seemed as proud of him as a good mother could be. When we weaned him, I took it upon myself to feed him but never gave him raw meat to eat, and he became so attached to me that he would not eat unless I was present but would whine and pine away until I returned when he would play like a kitten with the fringe of my sash, climb in my lap, and lick my hand.

Knowing now that my countrymen could soon return to Zion, I felt a heavy burden on my heart, realizing that many were not ready spiritually to rebuild Jerusalem and its Temple. It was now sixty-nine years since I had been brought captive to Babylon. In one year more, my people would be allowed to return. I read again and again in the book of Jeremiah the prophet that seventy years were to pass during the desolation of Jerusalem, and my spiritual burden for my people led me to intercede with God more urgently than ever in their behalf. I made a confession of our sin and an acknowledgment of God's righteousness. I acknowledged that the people had disobeyed God's law so wonderfully revealed to them, that they had been deaf to the words of the prophets whom God had sent to admonish them. I praised Him for His faithfulness and mercy and then besought Him that He would again turn in mercy instead of judgment to Jerusalem—not for our sake but for His sake so that glory might redound to His name; and while I was praying, the answer came, and Gabriel, the prince of God who had appeared to me in my vision of the river Ulai, predicted the time of Messiah's coming and of events that lay between the time of my prayer and the reign of the Promised One.

 During the reign of Nabonidus, many cities throughout the kingdom had been robbed of their particular deities; their images had been brought to Babylon with the idea that they would lend greater protection to the city and help to increase its glory among the nations of the earth. The result of this proliferation of idols in Babylon had hastened God's judgment upon the city, for there is nothing God hates worse than the worship of images of wood and stone, of precious metal and cast iron, the work of men's hands. The taking away of their special deities had angered cities throughout all Babylonia, and this was one thing that made them so susceptible to the overtures of Cyrus as he sought to win them away from their loyalties to Babylon and her monarchs. Cyrus's policy was to return them in triumphant procession to their former shrines, and he had issued a series of decrees guaranteeing complete freedom to each country and to each city to worship its own gods.

When he came to Babylon, he gave ready ear to the petition of the Hebrews that they be allowed to return to Zion and rebuild their temple there. Moreover, he undertook to bear the expenses of the construction of God's house from the royal treasury. The Hebrews accepted this graciously, but deep down believed it to be only right and just since the pillage of their homeland had so greatly enriched mighty Babylon.

It was, in a sense, the return of a people to their homeland from captivity, but in reality, very few who had been brought out in the captivity joined in the homeward journey. Many were dead, and those who remained were, for the most part, too feeble because of age to undertake the trip. Most of those who headed westward toward Jerusalem were the sons and grandsons and greatgrandsons of the original exiles.

Azariah's twin sons, now mature men, went back. In fact, Sheshbazzar, well known as a treasurer in the kingdom, signed the receipt for the vessels of God's house which were delivered into his custody as a prince of Judah.

Many of those who had been accustomed to visiting me as young men decided to go, taking with them, of course, their wives and children. Tel-Abib, for the most part, became a town of elderly people, except for the Babylonians to whom property had been sold and who now moved into what had formerly been an entirely Hebrew settlement.

The body of Meshach has now for some eight years rested beside that of Abednego in the Jewish cemetery. I have taken Shadrach, bedridden with his twisted joints and the pain in his back, to live with me. He is now unaware of his surroundings and prates constantly of his boyhood, all the years in Babylon forgotten. He is a child again playing in the fields near Bethlehem, or watching the soldiers maneuver on the parade ground outside the walls of Zion. I think, however, I miss Belzephon most of all. Leah and Rachel, forgetful old ladies, spend their time between naps at needlework, their eyes so dim they cannot see the patterns and, therefore, are blissfully unaware of the mistakes they make. I am almost ashamed of myself for being so active and possessing the full use of my faculties. I have to remind myself it is something for which I should give God the praise and not feel guilty and ashamed.

My will is made, and except for funds to provide for the care of these three old people who share the house with me and for the servants who have been so faithful, all my estate is to be divided between the twin sons of Azariah and the establishment of a school in Jerusalem to train teachers of the Law and the Prophets. I shall send a copy of the will together with this journal by the next royal courier to Abonizah, asking that he and his sons after him act as executors in this matter.

I sit here now upon the housetop, my eyes westward toward Jerusalem, Gubaru sleeping beside my chair. I think, perhaps, my nephews— for so I have come to call them since the time the queen mistakenly named them so—will find this journal of my days in Babylon a source of some interest, and I will have it finished before dawn. The BOOK, and that I name in capital letters, given me by the Spirit of the High God and set down in the words which He chose, is not finished yet and further revelations await, which I will not understand; but I will find them clear when the Great King reigns. The preservation of that Book I leave to Him whose Word it is. This one is mine, a human document.

I paused a moment here to glance back at the beginning of the Book, and all at once, I realize how far I have come. Gubaru, now wide awake, sits with his paw upon my knee and stares unblinkingly into the darkness beyond the circle of the lamplight where I know he sees the figure of the guardian, invisible to me.